Alfred Austin

The Poetry of the Period

Alfred Austin

The Poetry of the Period

ISBN/EAN: 9783742813848

Manufactured in Europe, USA, Canada, Australia, Japa

Cover: Foto ©Andreas Hilbeck / pixelio.de

Manufactured and distributed by brebook publishing software
(www.brebook.com)

Alfred Austin

The Poetry of the Period

THE
POETRY OF THE PERIOD.

BY

ALFRED AUSTIN,

AUTHOR OF

 SEASON: A SATIRE;" "THE HUMAN TRAGEDY," ETC.

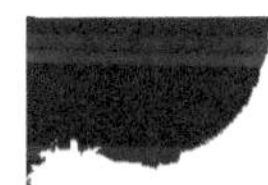

LONDON:

[R]ICHARD BENTLEY, NEW BURLINGTON STRE[ET,]

Publisher in Ordinary to Her Majesty.

1870.

All Rights Reserved.

TO

E. D. FORGUES,

ONE OF A BRILLIANT BAND OF LIVING FRENCH CRITICS,

TO WHOM, ALAS! WE POSSESS NO PARALLEL,

This Volume is Dedicated,

WITH

EVERY EXPRESSION OF ADMIRATION

AND

FRIENDLY REGARD.

ROME, *February*, 1870.

CONTENTS.

THE POETRY OF THE PERIOD.

Mr. Tennyson.

IF one were to enter a modern drawing-room filled with the average polite society of the day, and then and there were to pluck up courage to declare that Mr. Tennyson has no sound pretensions to be called a great poet, and will of a certainty not be esteemed such by an unbiassed posterity, I suppose he would not create more astonishment, or be regarded more unanimously as a heretic, than would another who in a company of *savans* expressed his doubts as to the law of gravitation, or a third who, before a committee of orthodox divines, exposed his utter disbelief in the inspiration of the Scriptures. Yet that, and nothing less, is the opinion to be

expounded in the ensuing pages, with a confidence equal to that I feel upon any subject I could name—a confidence not the growth of yesterday, but of long, deliberate, and ever-deepening conviction. It is indeed high time that somebody should speak out what is, to my knowledge, distinctly in the minds of an independent few, and, I have reason to suspect, hazily in the minds of the servile many. The age in which we live is, in the formation of opinion, if not absolutely in the expression of it, such an oppressive one, the conventional sense of the majority so overpowers the critical sense of the discriminating minority, that when an opinion has, in the phraseology of the day, once " turned the corner " and got itself accepted by a preponderance of voices, it is almost hopeless to think of reversing it. So hopeless is it that, as a rule, no one ever expends his energy in the attempt; or, if he does, his spoken or written efforts are relegated to the obscure pages of some neglected publication, which either expires of its eccentricity, or obtains a licence of vitality by surrendering its independence of judgment, and proclaiming in a still more extravagant key the sentiments it began by struggling to stem. So

has it been by the national estimate formed of
Mr. Tennyson. It would not be easy to name
the precise moment at which it was settled once
and for all that he is a great poet, though I am
inclined to think that the period might be marked
by the publication of the " Idylls of the King."
The point, however, is not one of very great
importance, except as showing—as I shall have
occasion to point out farther on—that his fame
has steadily increased precisely as his genuine
poetical power has steadily waned. What I wish
to emphasize at present is, that his being a great
poet is now regarded as an established fact. It
is esteemed to be beyond the reach of criticism,
and the vulgar suppose that nobody for a moment
dreams of challenging it. I am going not only
to challenge it, but to deny it altogether, and to
implore the age, whilst there yet is time, to
save itself by a seasonable recantation from the
posthumous ridicule and contempt in which a
conventional persistence in an untenable opinion
of permanent interest will necessarily involve it.

We are so perniciously given in these days to
extravagance of all sorts, and notably to extravagance of language—so frivolously addicted to
excessive censure and unmeasured laudation—

that all sense of accuracy seems to be deserting
us. Ten years ago, anything that pleased, from
a bonnet to an epic, was "charming." Five
years ago, it was "so charming." Now it is
"too charming." I mention these phrases as
illustrative, and as proving the stringent necessity of calling the reader's attention to what
it is exactly that is asserted, and what it is
exactly that is denied. My proposition is, that Mr.
Tennyson is not a great poet, unquestionably not a
poet of the first rank, all but unquestionably not
a poet of the second rank, and probably—though
no contemporary perhaps can settle that—not
even at the head of poets of the third rank, among
whom he must ultimately take his place. The
prevailing or universally expressed opinion on the
subject is, that he is a great poet, a very great
poet, perhaps as great a poet as ever lived, the
latchet of whose shoe Dryden would not be
worthy to tie; greater than Scott, greater than
Shelley, greater than Keats, greater than Wordsworth, greater than Byron—yes, ever so much
greater than Byron—certainly as great as Milton
or Spenser, and only not quite named in the same
breath with Shakespeare, because the self-same
mingled academical and drawing-room conven-

tionality, which places him in a sphere preposterously beyond his real deserts, allows nobody to be *par aut secundus* to our mighty dramatist. I do not mean to say that in the second instance conventionality, and sound criticism are not at one; but if the latter had not succeeded in compelling the adherence of the former already, and before Mr. Tennyson's claims had been mooted, I entertain no doubt whatever that even Shakespeare's superiority would not have been safe against the ignorant intrusion into his society by the Poet Laureate's worshippers of their paraded idol. But short of Shakespeare, it is certain there is no English bard with whom they do not presume continually to compare him, and almost invariably to the disadvantage of the mighty dead. This is the opinion I challenge and denounce—the opinion that will make posterity shriek with laughter and flout us with scorn.

Nobody, I presume, will contest the statement that no man can make himself a great poet by writing a large quantity of mediocre poetry, or a certain quantity of unsurpassable excellence in expression. Otherwise two men of very different merit, Blackmore and Gray, would both be great poets. Just as in Roman Catholic theology no amount of venial sins will constitute one mortal one, so according to the canons of poetry no amount of pretty, beautiful, tender, elegant, thoughtful verse, can constitute its author a mighty singer. If Mr. Tennyson be a great poet, where is his great subject greatly sung? Where is his "Hamlet," his "Lear," his "Faëry Queen," his "Paradise Lost," his "Prometheus Unbound," his "Cenci," his "Cain," his "Manfred," his "Childe Harold," —ay, his "Endymion," or his "Marmion?" He had his great subject once, and once only, and, in vulgar parlance, he "funked" it. What has he made of his "Flos Regum Arthurus?" Four* exquisite cabinet pictures; but that is all. You prefer cabinet pictures? Be it so. But neither four, nor forty, nor four hundred of them, constitute a *magnum opus*, or their producer a mighty artificer, or in any sense the peer of one who is. If "King Arthur" and the "Table Round" could not, under favourable circumstances, be woven into the substance of a really great poem, never was the subject that could. No doubt Mr. Tennyson is as well aware of that fact as anybody; and the consciousness of it governed him

---

* Now extended to eight.

in his original selection of it. He kept revolving it for years, in the fond hope that a due poetic treatment of it would make his laurelled head. strike the stars; but eventually he had to own that he was unequal to the glorious task. The subject was too much for him. *Non ex quovis ligno fit Mercurius.* The stuff of a great poet was not in him; and he confessed as much— perhaps not quite consciously, but still, we may be sure, with a pang of mortification, when he abandoned a lofty but illusory aim, and contented himself with executing four charming and highly finished fragments or driblets, in the shape of " Enid," " Elaine," " Vivien," and " Guinevere." Never was there a poet with such sound judgment and good common sense as Mr. Tennyson. He takes, and has always taken, his own measure far more accurately than his silly and immoderate admirers. He has never yet attempted anything beyond his reach; and the consequence is, he has never conspicuously failed. But is it not he himself who reminds us that

" He is all fault who hath no fault at all " ?

The same holds good of the small poet, whom unwise voices want to proclaim great. There is no really great poet that has not written unmitigated nonsense, perpetrated notable fiascos—that does not, in a word, abound with faults.   Where are Mr. Tennyson's faults ?   He has only one— the fault of not being great enough to commit any.   He has what Mr. Carlyle has so happily described as " the completeness of a limited mind."   He never stumbles, for he never runs.   He never flags, because he never soars. He never rises into air too rarefied for him, as Shelley does—air so light and fine that even wings do not there support him.   He knows what he can do, and he does it.   It is delicate, subtle, pathetic, sometimes even solemn; it is anything else you like; but it is never great.

It is not the purpose of this present paper to note what Mr. Tennyson is, but rather what he is not.   Yet the second point cannot well be established without the first being, to a certain degree, entertained.   His first little volume of poems, published in 1830, could not by any possibility, even in the worst and most uncritical of times, have made a poetical reputation; and, whatever folks now affect to think of them, they were thought very little of when they first appeared.   Byron had been dead only six years—

we fear he would have poked shocking fun at them, with their Adelines, Madelines, and Lilians, had he been alive—and the generation that had fed on his strong meat was not prepared all of a sudden to smack its lips over food for babes. Yet there was genuine poetry in one or two of them—of course of a rather small sort, and though happy twists of expression were more noticeable in them than any more substantial quality. But, besides betokening in the author an airy fancy and a rare delicacy of touch, they prompted the expectation of something better than themselves. That something better—very decidedly better—came two years later. There was still a rather namby-pamby "sweet pale Margaret," recalling the Madelines and Adelines of the previous volume; but there were likewise the "Dream of Fair Women," the "Palace of Art," "Œnone," and the "Lotos Eaters;" and what was more important to most people, and is to this day, there were in it "New Year's Eve," the "Miller's Daughter," and "Lady Clara Vere de Vere." There could be no doubt in any reasonable mind that the author was a poet, and a poet of no mean order. Ten years passed away; and in 1842 came the "Talking Oak," "Locksley Hall," and those blank verse English Idylls which sounded the key-note of nearly all Mr. Tennyson's latest and more extensive poetic labours. He has added no fresh poetic laurels, *in kind,* to his brow since that date. As far as quality is concerned, there are to be found in those first three volumes, now published as one under the simple name of " Poems," types of everything he has since written, and types equal to anything that has followed. I am not forgetting " Maud "*— the weakest and worst, despite its several beauties, of Mr. Tennyson's works—nor " In Memoriam," in the opinion of many people, though certainly not in mine, his strongest and best. " Maud " is a *pot pourri* of his various manners, each of which is plainly discernible in some one page or other of the " Poems." The

---

* In an article written by a distinguished French critic in the " Revue des Deux Mondes," February 15, 1869, entitled " Un Retour vers Byron," occurs the following passage : " Aujourd'hui même les 'admirables passages de Byron contre la guerre n'ont rien perdu de leur puissance. Aujourd'hui *Maud* est à peu pres oublié; ou est toujours transporté des chaudes peintures de la prise d'Ismaïl. La verité seule est durable, et Byron l'a rencontrée." These remarks are by M. Louis Etienne; but if the reader wishes to see what the impartial " foreign friend" thinks of Mr. Tennyson, let him read M. Taine. In fact, Mr. Tennyson is only an English poet, and never will be anything more. That is another note of his comparative inferiority.

key of "In Memoriam" was first struck in the verses beginning, "You ask me why, though ill at ease," published in 1832. But I take 1842 as the climacteric. No higher note has been struck by Mr. Tennyson since, and by far his best notes have since then wholly deserted him. It is pretty certain that no posterity, however distant, will allow the "Talking Oak," or "Locksley Hall" to die; but the English Idylls, if they survive far into the next century, will survive in an academical sense only, as Thomson's "Seasons," or Young's "Night Thoughts" do now. "In Memoriam" will assuredly be handed over to the dust as soon as a generation arises which has come to its senses, or even to a tolerable notion of what it is aiming at, in religious and spiritual thought. Passages no doubt will be saved, as they will from "Maud," and from the "Idylls of the King," but their very survival will doom the text from which they are selected to practical oblivion. As for the "Princess," such is even already its fate. Its pretty little·songs and a well-known passage at the close of the poem are being perpetually quoted, only to prove what a trivial impression, if any, has been created in the general mind by its other innumerable pages. All of them alike are already manifestly destined to be, *as complete poems*, to dumb forgetfulness a prey; and all of them for the same reason—their length, though by no means excessive when poems of any pretension are spoken of, is so conspicuously greater than their excellence. Their weight is too much for their momentum, and consequently they will fall short and soon. If you want to be heard afar off, you must shout, not loud or long, but *high.* Mr. Tennyson's poetical pitch is not high enough—he cannot make it high enough—and the inevitable consequence is that posterity will not hear him, save in little snatches or breaks of voice, as it still hears Cowley or Falconer.

Still if it could be shown that Mr. Tennyson —though he has written no single great work, no one poem sufficiently sublime in conception and execution to defy the destructiveness of Time—has given frequent or even occasional utterance to really great poetical thoughts, or to poetical images really sublime, it might perhaps be impossible, and it would certainly be churlish, to refuse him the title, by courtesy at least, of a great poet. It is true that single-speech Hamilton does not usually figure in the list of English orators, nor is Earl Russell regarded as a famous epigrammatist, because he once made the exceedingly happy remark that proverbs are the wisdom of many and the wit of one. Nevertheless, though I could not waive the important point on which I have been insisting, I would not press it, if sublimity of idea could be indicated as ever and anon rising out of the usually tame and scarcely undulating level of Mr. Tennyson's compositions. But, with an intimate acquaintance with everything he has written, and after long and deliberate reflection and search, I have no hesitation in saying that, in the whole range of his poetry, there is not to be found even a solitary instance of a sublime thought sublimely expressed. In really great poets—in Shakespeare, Byron, Shelley — such thoughts crowd upon us thick and fast—pelt us, in fact, with their prodigal frequency. They smite us, stun us, take away our breath, make us bow our heads and wonder, fancying that we have seen over into the other world—had a glimpse of the supernatural, a flash of the Eternal. But Mr. Tennyson! He is sweet, tender, touching, polished—his is the *perpolita oratio*—a gentleman, a scholarly writer, a more highly-finished

oneself, so to speak, but never the man "who
has seen Hell," or any of the non-visible things
of the universe.   He is not even the *gran maestro,*
of whom anybody can say

> "........ da cui io tolsi
> Lo bello stile che m' ha fatto onore."

Many have imitated him, it is true, and most
successfully; but who has gained special honour
by it?   Names need not be mentioned; anybody
can suggest them for himself; but his metrical
disciples have been so numerous, have copied
their original so amazingly well, and their excellence in this respect has been the subject of
such general remark, that Mr. Tennyson has
thereby been betrayed into one of the few un-
dignified acts of his singularly self-respecting
and honourable life.   Unwisely stung by the
observation that his works were objectionably
easy of imitation, he has retorted in some stupid
little verses to the effect that all can grow the
flower now that they have got the seed, which
came originally from his garden.   The conceit is
pretty, and quite in the author's style; but used
as an argument, for which it is intended, it is
not only sophistical—it is damning to the person

that employs it. Let us accept the metaphor, and use it in this further inquiry: Who has grown Shaksperean flowers of poesy?—flowers such as Byron's, that he did not cultivate, but coaxed, like Spring, with a smile, or drew, like hot Summer, with the warmth of imperious passion, from the mountain side?—flowers such as Shelley has scattered broadcast through his pages?—flowers such as he himself speaks of in language whose very syllables distil the wild-honied poetry of no fabled Hymettus?—flowers such as

> " Daisies, those pale arcturi of the earth,
>   The constellated flower that never sets" ?

or such as

> . . . . . " the tender harebell, at whose birth
>   The sod scarce heaved" ?

Who has got the seed of these, and grown their duplicates? Who has imitated any of these three? No one, and for the simple reason that nobody can. Mr. Tennyson does well to speak of "his garden." There it is! His flowers of poesy are flowers of the garden—a beautiful, exquisite, tasteful, sweet-smelling, brightly-glittering garden, but—a garden. And gardens and

all that they produce are essentially imitable.
There may be only one Sir Joseph Paxton and
only one Chatsworth, but their imitators run
them hard. Similarly, Mr. Tennyson's may still
be the best as it was the first garden of its sort,
and he deserves, like Paxton and Chatsworth,
the honour due and invariably rendered to pre-
cursors. But it is of the very essence of truly
great poetry that it can neither be invented,
cultivated, nor copied. It grows of itself in a
certain soil, and it will grow in no other, let
metrical floriculturists labour as deftly as ever
they will. It is an affair, not of grafting,
crossing, fertilizing, or of ordinary reproduction
at all, but of spontaneous generation, or what we
call such in default of knowledge whence this
strange, fitful, efflorescent foliage comes. The
birds drop it, the winds bring it, the heavens
rain it, the mist and the storm-clouds carry it
about. It germinates in the rays of the sun, in
the beams of the watery moon, in the secrecy
and shroud of unfathomable darkness. It comes
of the breath of God. Let there be light! And,
lo! there is light and a poet! It has nothing
to do with gardens and garden seeds, trim parterres, new variations, and watering-pots. There

lies the whole difference between great poets and poets that are not great—between Mr. Tennyson and the Di Majores. And as there is a difference between them not only intensely of degree, but even of kind, so is there a difference in their doom. Garden poetry, besides being imitable, is variable, and subject to fashion, whim, caprice. Now Dutch gardening is in vogue, as it was when Pope* wrote. Now Italian gardening is all the rage, as it was when Cowper trimly moralized. Now English landscape-gardening ousts both, and Mr. Tennyson comes to the front. But Shakespeare, Byron, Shelley, have nothing to do with gardens and gardening. Their concern is with the permanent aspects of Nature—human nature included; with the sea, the sky, the mountains, the far-stretching landscape, stormy winds that fulfil His Word, the planets, the intolerable thunder, grim murder, vaulting ambition, mad revenge, earthquakes, and Promethean discontent. These are enduring. No fashion can change the waves and waters, no mode move the mountains, no alteration of taste

---

* Pope, however, like Lucretius, has made his peace with posterity, and saved himself from all peril of oblivion, by writing a great ethical poem—a possession for ever—the "Essay on Man.'

obliterate the stars. These are always the selfsame, and their years shall not fail. So are
their singers. Where are the gardens of Sallust?
Where the fountains of Mæcenas? Where the
terraces and laurelled walks of Hadrian?

> " Cypress and ivy, weed and wallflower grown
> Matted and massed together."

These survive, and would still survive, even if
the ruins on which they feed had been consumed.
The Sabine hills are there, so are the Alban, so
is the Campagna. You can kill neither the gods
nor Nature, nor the inspired voices that are
divinely commissioned to speak of them to their
fellows. But mere man and his tricks and
fancies, his little comedies and lesser tragedies;
his fashions, poses, and conceits; his Adelines,
Madelines, and Enoch Ardens, well enough for
their little day, necessarily pass away, and with
them the gentle, elegant, but ephemeral creatures
that have twittered about them on the particular
guitar of the period.

The more one considers this garden metaphor
and all that it suggests, the more applicable it
ever seems to be to Mr. Tennyson as a poet, and
the more satisfactorily explanatory of his exact

poetical position, and its relation to that occupied by those with whom he has been so unwisely, and indeed sillily, compared. Let me quote a beautiful passage from the " Gardener's Daughter," to my thinking the best of his Idylls :—

> " Not wholly in the busy world, nor quite
>   Beyond it, blooms the garden that I love.
>   News from the humming city comes to it
>   In sound of funeral or of marriage bells ;
>   And, sitting muffled in dark leaves, you hear
>   The windy clanging of the minster clock ;
>   Although between it and the garden lies
>   A league of grass, washed by a slow broad stream,
>   That, stirred with languid pulses of the oar,
>   Waves all its lazy lilies,* and creeps on,
>   Barge-laden, to three arches of a bridge
>   Crown'd with the minster-towers.
>   The fields between
>   Are dewy-fresh, browsed by deep-uddered kine,
>   And all about the large lime feathers low,
>   The lime a summer home of murmurous wings."†

You like that vastly ! It is one of your favourite passages ! So it is with me—especially because it is so intensely Tennysonian, and marks in a definite manner his powers, his mission—in a word, his sweep. I will illustrate and enlarge

---

* A bit of plagiarism from Shelley, by the way.

† Again, copied from Keats, and spoiled in the copying.

on my meaning in a moment. But let me first
ask, *à propos* of your admiring the above passage
so warmly, in what sense it is you admire it, and
to what extent? You like it immensely! But
what do you *think of it?* Do you seriously think
it equal to, or worthy to be named in the same
poetical breath with the thunderstorm in the
Jura in "Childe Harold," the description of
Waterloo, the long-sustained wail over the "lone
mother of dead Empires, the Niobe of Nations,"
the address, as of an equal, to the Ocean? equal
to or fit to be mentioned in the same poetical
breath with the best-known quotations from
"Lear," "Measure for Measure," "Henry the
Fourth," "A Midsummer Night's Dream," or
with the most glittering passages from "Alastor,"
the "Lament for Adonaïs," the "Revolt of
Islam," or the "Prometheus Unbound?" Do
you think *that?* No, but you like it better; it
comes home to you more; you care more for it?
Be it so. Perhaps, too, you prefer the canter of
your mamma's steady nag to the long stride and
tremendous bound of your father's thorough-
bred? But which, after all, is the better horse
of the two? We dare say you prefer Zephyrus
to Eurus; but which is the stronger, grander

wind? The first is smoother, softer, and more in harmony with your mood. That is quite conceivable. But what is your mood? An amiable, elegant, refined one, truly and obviously. But an heroic one?—a sublime one?—a great one? Scarcely. Yet it cannot be supposed that, because you are so constituted as to have a personal preference for the less, you do not know the difference between the less and the greater, and mistake the one for the other. Like Mr. Tennyson, by all means; it would be the height of stupidity and intolerance to try to prevent your doing so. All that is asked is, that you should confess you think a great deal more of poets whom you care to read a good deal less. To refuse that much would imply only obstinacy or dullness, and place you among your favourite poet's " purblind race of miserable men," who " take true for false, or false for true."

But quitting the ground of mere individual predilection, which, as we have seen, goes for absolutely nothing in a correct estimate of the relative grandeur of poets, let us revert to our quotation, and scrutinize it as it illustrates what I have termed the " sweep " of its author. I have said that it is intensely Tennysonian. It is the poet speaking not so much from his heart as from his whole nature :—

> " Not wholly in the busy world, nor quite
> Beyond it, blooms the garden that I love."

What a mine of confession and suggestiveness there is in those two lines, when we come to consider and accurately measure the genius of their author! From the fulness of the heart the mouth speaketh, and his heart is partly in the city and partly in the fields. He is too much of a poet to be enamoured of Rotten Row or Piccadilly, or to be able to exclaim, " Give *me* the sunny side of Pall Mall;" but he is not enough of a poet, not exclusively such, so as to be able to exclaim :—

> " With me,
> High mountains are a feeling, but the hum
> Of human cities torture."

It is a different lyre that strikes out that discontented note. Mr. Tennyson avows that he loves " news from the humming city," and does not like to get too far away from it. And when he does, where does he wish to find himself? Among the mountains? Anywhere but there! I do not remember a single earnest allusion to high mountains in the whole of his poems. They are not with him a feeling. They are too much for him. If he confronted them, he feels instinctively they would silence him. Wordsworth, the sublime and holy, awed by them, yet competent, like Moses, to bring down from them to the vulgar world the lessons they command in fire of sunset or thunder of storm, fled to them as companions, not without sense of dread, but imperiously drawn to their tops by inspiration and worship :—

> " The sounding cataract
> Haunted me like a passion : the tall rock,
> The mountain, and the deep and gloomy wood,
> Their colours and their forms, were then to me
> An appetite; a feeling and a love
> That had no need of a remoter charm,
> By thought supplied, nor any interest
> Unborrowed from the eye."

Again, in the " Excursion," the same lofty voice smites our ears as with tidings from that land of " light that never was on sea or shore :"—

> " The solid frame of earth
> And ocean's liquid mass in gladness lay
> Beneath him. Far and wide the clouds were touched,
> And in their silent faces could be read
> Unutterable love. *Sound needed none,*
> *Nor any sense of joy."*

No need of "news from the humming city."
No need of "sound of funeral or of marriage
bells." No need of "the windy clanging of the
minster clock :"—

> "Sound needed none,
> Nor any sense of joy; his spirit drank
> The spectacle: sensation, soul, and form
> All melted into him; they swallowed up
> His animal being; in them did he live,
> And by them did he live; they were his life.
> In such access of mind, in such high hour
> Of visitation from the living God,
> Thought was not; in enjoyment it expired."

I have preferred to quote from Wordsworth,
because it would be a bold thing to insist, despite
the unsurpassed sublimity of these passages, that
he is, taken all in all, a poet of the very
highest order, and because it never enters the
vulgar mind to suppose that he is a far greater
poet than Mr. Tennyson. I wish Mr. Moxon
would tell us what proportion there is between
his sale, during the last twenty-five years, of the
works of the two men. The figures would show
the estimation in which they are held, respectively, by the critical crowds of the age. But I
defy Mr. Tennyson's admirers to quote anything
from his works fit for one moment to be com-

pared as sublime—in other words, as great
poetry—with the lines just printed; and there
are many more of them equally sublime in the
two particular passages from which they are
taken. The challenge is of course unanswerable,
or can be answered only by Mr. Tennyson's
preference for

> " A league of grass, washed by a slow broad stream,
>   That, stirred with languid pulses of the oar,
>   Waves all its lazy lilies, and creeps on,
>   Barge-laden, to three arches of a bridge
>   Crown'd with the minster-towers."

Who does not feel that we have dropped to
a lower key — from " sounding cataracts " to
"languid pulses of the oar"—from storm-winds
to zephyrs—from thunder-fugues to " clanging
clocks ?" I have nothing to say against it. It
is exceedingly pretty, soothing, elegant; but it
is not grand. It is the poetry of the drawing-
room, not the music of the Spheres.

Nor will it avail to plead that Wordsworth
goes on to confess

> "That time is past,
> And all its aching joys are now no more,
> And all its dizzy raptures.
> . . . . I have learned
> To look on Nature not as in the hour

> Of thoughtless youth; but hearing oftentimes
> The still sad music of humanity."

For the lines that follow show what was the real change that had come over him, enabling him oftentimes to hear this still sad music of humanity. No man is a great poet who does not hear it, and who confines himself to singing of Nature alone. It is the poet's loftiest mission to blend the two, but to blend them in so subtle a manner that the mystery of the one deepens the mystery of the other, and makes them almost interchangeable; to produce, in fact, that

> " Sense sublime
> Of something far more deeply interfused,"

of which Wordsworth speaks in the selfsame passage. Mr. Tennyson knows nothing of this. He writes " of funeral and of marriage bells," as novelists do, and he writes of "a vapour from the margin, blackening over heath and holt," as poets of a certain order do; but even these he does not contrive to commingle in such a way as to bring before us the everlasting puzzlo of the sympathy, and yet conflict, of Humanity with Nature.

"Drug thy memories, lest thou learn it, lest thy heart bo
  put to proof,
In the dead unhappy night, and when the rain is on
  the roof,"

is his nearest approach to it that I can recall;
and this, though an exceedingly happy touch,
has in it no element of real grandeur or sublime
pathos. What is it compared to Byron's touch
about Spring-coming,

"With all her joyous birds upon the wing,
  I turned from all she brought to those she could
    not bring."

Here we have Man, Nature, and the Perpetual
Mystery face to face; no shrinking on any side,
and the poet giving adequate voice and expression to all :—

"Not that I love Man less, but Nature more,
  From these our interviews, in which I steal
  From what I may be, or have been before,
  To mingle with the Universe, and feel
What I can not express, yet cannot all conceal."

It is in such passages as these that we are
lifted up, just as we are in Shakespeare's magnificent lines :—

"To be embodied in the viewless winds,
  And blown with restless violence round about
  The pendent world :"

and are made to feel that even we, like the wizard hands that thus for a moment exalt us, are, as Shelley says, "made one with Nature." But what mighty pinions are required for such empyrean flights as these! In one of Lacordaire's most magnificent sermons, preached upon the text, "Go and convert all nations," he winds up an impassioned passage concerning apostolic zeal and the missionary spirit, by exclaiming, "Go across the mountains and the seas! Go, but go straight! Go, as the eagles go, and the angels!" Poets should, and great poets do, go in such a fashion. They go — like the eagles! They mount, ride on the storm, scale the ether, calm or disturbed, and stare at the sun. They go— like the angels! You cannot shut them out of heaven. You cannot exclude them from the deepest fathoms of the sea. For them, however it may be with kings, there is no "Thus far, and no farther" .... "I have loved thee, ocean .... I am, as it were, a child of thee .... I lay my hand upon thy mane .... Thou dost bound beneath me, as a steed that knows its rider." What splendid familiarity!—familiarity like that which enabled Shakespeare too to write :—

" . . . . I have bedimm'd
The noontide sun, call'd forth the mutinous winds,
And 'twixt the green sea and the azur'd vault
Set roaring war: to the dread rattling thunder
Have I given fire, and rifted Jove's stout oak
With his own bolt: the strong-bas'd promontory
Have I made shake; and by the spurs pluck'd up
The pine and cedar . . . .
By my so potent art."

Ay, there it is! "By my so potent art." If we could imagine Shakespeare, Byron, and even Wordsworth, meeting in the Elysian Fields, can we doubt that the "one touch of nature," common, as we have briefly shown, to all three, would make them kin, and force them to recognize each other as master-minds? But Mr. Tennyson! I fear Shakespeare would consider he had too much of the "pouncet-box" about him. They would relegate him to "the garden that he loves," and regard him as one who, like his own "slow broad stream," is stirred only with languid pulses. His muse is dainty and delicious, but it is not daring and defiant. It is Pegasus, and Pegasus with four very decent legs, small, elegant head, right well groomed, and with an uncommonly good mane and tail; but it is Pegasus without wings. It would be cruel to apply to him Lacordaire's splendid image. Alas! he is no eagle. As I have said, he never soars. He twitters under our roof, sweeps and skims round and round our ponds, is musical in the branches of our trees, plumes himself on the edges of our fountains, builds himself a warm nest under our gables and even in our hearts, "cheeps," to use his own words, "twenty million loves," feeds out of our hand, eyes us askance, struts along our lawns, and flutters in and out among our flowery parterres—does all, in fact, that welcome, semi-domesticated swallows, linnets, and musical bullfinches do; but there it ends. He is no "scorner of the ground." He never leaves us to plunge among the far-off precipitous crags, to commune with embryonic tempests, to travel with the planets, and then swoop down divinely laden with messages hard yet not altogether impossible to understand. We love him, because he is ours. We love him, because, like the garden he himself loves, he is "not wholly in the busy world, nor quite beyond it."

In other words, he thinks with us of this particular day, feels with us of this day, and is the exponent of such poetical feelings as in this day we are capable of. But as far

as poetry is concerned we and our day are
not great, but little, and he shares our little-
ness with us.   It is not our fault, some may
perhaps think it is not even our misfortune, that
such greatness as the present age achieves, or
can achieve, does not lie in the poetical, but in a
wholly opposite direction.   The age is scientific
or it is nothing.   Now science and all its processes, its aims and its methods alike, are antagonistic to poetry, and its aims and methods.   The
scope of science, as far as literature is concerned,
is demonstration, and its machinery must be
strict reasoning of some sort.   The scope of
poetry is the embodiment of emotion, and its
vehicle and means must be of an unreasoning,
and sometimes even of an unreasonable character.
Greater contrast, indeed more absolute conflict,
could not well be imagined.   Mr. Tennyson has
been the complete sport of this conflict; with
what results anybody who is well acquainted with
his works and has this key to guide him may
soon perceive for himself.   He is alternately the
poet pure and simple, singing true songs, sweet
or sad, as it happens; or the poet crossed by the
man of scientific thought and intelligence, trying
to weld together two things that are essentially

antagonistic, and producing a species of metrical emulsion that people with only poetical instincts feel not to be poetry, and people with only scientific insight know not to be science, but which people with lingering poetical tastes and growing scientific proclivities combined would like to make serve both for poetry and science. Men with a strong poetical turn of mind, but with not so decided and obstinate a bias for being poets as Mr. Tennyson, give up the struggle, consciously or unconsciously, and become—like Professor Tyndall or Mr. Disraeli—philosophers or politicians. Men, on the contrary, with the same turn, but with a still more decided, obstinate, and exclusive poetical nature and temperament than Mr. Tennyson, squander their lives in trying to attain the impossible, exhaust themselves in poetical spasms, and illustrate Alexander Smith's simile :—

> "O Poesy! thou art a rock;
> I, a weak wave, would break on thee, and die."

I could name one or two living men who have achieved considerable notoriety by their volumes of verse, whom it would be easy to imagine being, in an age more favourable to the achievement, poets of the very highest order. I feel sure that Mr. Tennyson could never have been that in any age, and probably never in any age a greater poet than he has proved himself in this. Yet, to the impartial mind, there can be no doubt that, as far as work done goes, the one or two men to whom I allude are very much his inferiors. And it is no paradox to say that their natural superiority to him is the very cause of their inferiority. Success, and even merit, as far as we can judge it, is the composite result of the agent and his conditions; and if the larger and grander agent be more out of harmony with the conditions under which he works than the smaller agent, it is not only possible, but almost certain, that the latter will produce more valuable work. To put an extreme but conclusive case. If Shakespeare had been living now, would he have been as great a poet as Mr. Tennyson is? I entertain little doubt that he would not, and I have serious doubt whether he would have been known as a poet at all worth speaking of. A pigmy can live and breathe in a place and atmosphere in which a giant could not move for want of room, or speak for want of air. Let us reverse the case. If Mr. Tennyson had been born in the Elizabethan era, should we ever have heard of him? Perhaps; but at most as the author of some courtly masques.

The truth is, the present age, taken in the lump, likes Mr. Tennyson's poetry, as any, and every age, has liked its particular poet, because he speaks its mind for it far more efficiently than anybody else. Consequently it likes and enjoys him better than Scott, better than Shelley, better than Byron, better than Milton, and—whatever it may now and then pretend to the contrary, out of sham and conventional deference—it likes and enjoys him better than Shakespeare. It reads him more, and gets more satisfaction out of reading him. But, as I said before, liking and enjoyment of a poet are no test of that poet's greatness. There are men of sound intellect and sense who infinitely prefer Horace to Homer, and women of exquisite sentiment who infinitely prefer Mrs. Hemans to Mrs. Barrett Browning. It so happens, however, that the serious critic can put himself outside folks' various likings and preferences. He is not bound by the average tastes of his time. All literature is open to him, and he approaches the measurement of any new poetical claimant with the standard left by the productions of bygone centuries. He does not ask men to give up their newly-found idol, the cherished poetical god of their narrow domestic hearth; but he does and must insist that they shall not mistake him for a celestial, and most of all that they shall not thoughtlessly or presumptuously call him Jove. If they do, he must produce his god-measurer, and reduce their little divinity to his true proportions.

It is natural enough that the age, having got in Mr. Tennyson a poet that it vastly likes, should want to persuade itself that he is a great poet. Self-love impels it to nourish the delusion. Nobody will deny that ours is a particularly vainglorious age; and, being such, it would be painful to it to confess that it has not produced a first-rate specimen of what it has hitherto been the universal creed to believe the highest mental type of humanity—viz., a really great poet. How do we note the past ages? ` We speak of the age of Homer, the age of Dante, the age of Shakespeare. Can anybody in his senses imagine posterity speaking of our age as the age of Tennyson? Posterity will be too kind to do anything so sardonic. It will speak of it as the age of Railways, the age of Destructive Criticism, or the age of Penny Papers. In some way or other it will try to distinguish us. But the age of Tennyson ! The notion is, of course, preposterous. If, then, this age of ours does not wish to cease to pride itself upon its achievements, and cannot make up its mind to lay aside its vaingloriousness, let it strive to persuade itself that great poetry is by no means the best and highest outcome of human genius. Let it turn round and assert that the Submarine Telegraph is grander than "Lear," the Pneumatic Dispatch grander than "Comus," Great Exhibitions grander than the "Tragedies of Æschylus," and the halfpenny "Echo" a greater triumph for man than the fourth canto of "Childe Harold." It is an intelligible position ; I do not say it is an indefensible one, though I confess I would rather not have to defend it. But, at any rate, let it either do that, and justify its vaingloriousness and conceit of superiority over all its predecessors by pointing to something in which it has unquestionably and immeasurably surpassed them, or let it stick to the old doctrine that a great poet is the crown and summit of an age's glory, and meekly confess that, though it has done its best, it has failed to produce one. But let it not make itself a laughing-stock to an irreverent posterity by piquing itself on what it has not got. We laugh at the contemporaries of Hayley. Do we want to be laughed at by our grandchildren? Mr. Tennyson is much more of a poet than Hayley, no doubt; but then Hayley was never belauded as Mr. Tennyson is by us. There is yet time to revise and recall our hasty and extravagant praises; and Mr. Tennyson's merits are so obvious and so considerable that, when we have plucked off all the false feathers in which we have bedecked him, some very beautiful plumage will remain. But our attempts to glorify ourselves by over-exalting him can do no possible good to anybody; and if we persist in this ridiculous course, it will only ensure our being scoffed at by less partial times as a parcel of indiscriminating dunces.

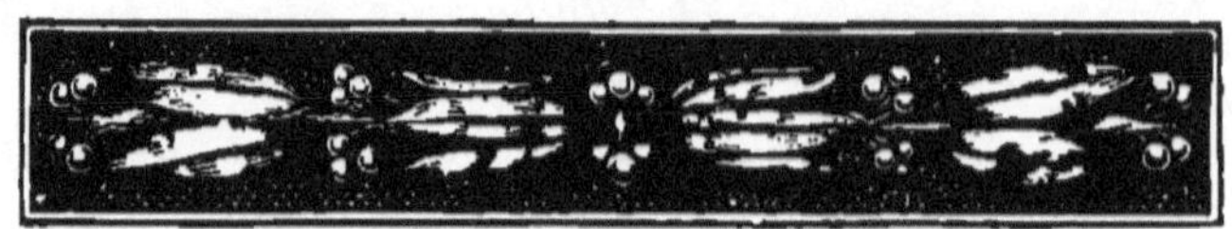

Mr. Browning.

THE soundness of an opinion may usually be tested by the amount of deliberation with which it is adopted, plus the tenacity with which, when so formed, it is adhered to. Men often arrive at conclusions with amazing haste, and maintain them with proportionate obstinacy; whilst others, who reach them after long consideration, abandon them almost as soon as they have been embraced. It is obvious that no reliance can be placed on views attended in either case with circumstances of so much suspicion. There exists a strong presumption of their validity only when they have been cautiously formed, and are consistently upheld.

The opinion which has prevailed during the last twelve years or so as to Mr. Tennyson's merits, does not satisfy one, at least, of these conditions. I will not stop to inquire how it came about that he was ever spoken of, by people who aspire to be authorities in such matters, as a great poet.* It is more to our present purpose to note the fact that even now, whilst he still lives, and his adulators are naturally averse from stultifying themselves by recanting the more fulsome praises they have so often and so confidently lavished on him, our Poet Laureate is beginning to totter on his throne. The signs of mutiny against his long unchallenged supremacy are unmistakable. I have already expressed tho opinion that, as far

---

* Simultaneously with the appearance of the foregoing paper on Mr. Tennyson in the " Temple Bar" magazine, appeared an article in the " Quarterly Review" on " Modern Poets," in which much the same view, though more guardedly worded, was taken of that gentleman's poetical position as is developed in my essay. Indeed there is a striking similarity between some of the illustrations employed in them to illustrate the fundamental difference between exquisite poetry and great poetry. I can therefore have no quarrel with the Quarterly Reviewer on that score. But I am lost in wonder at a writer, who has evidently some breadth of judgment and some insight into the subject, quoting the following lines (from Mr. Hugh Arthur Clough, deceased, whom certain pedants have been striving for the last seven or eight years to induce the British public to accept as a bard, and, indeed, a bard of no small magnitude) as poetry, and observing that he doubts " if a more perfect description

as work done is concerned, he is unquestionably
at the head of living English poets. But in the
quarters whence first issued, and where was long
stoutly maintained, the preposterous theory that
he is a really great poet, voices scarcely ambiguous proceed, intimating not only that there
is perhaps some doubt upon that point, but that
in any case one greater than he has long been
dwelling amongst us. For let there be no mistake about it. The same coteries, and in many
cases the very same people, who by dint of per-

of the surroundings of a waterfall can be found anywhere."
Here it is :—

> " But in the interval here the boiling pent-up water
> Frees itself by a final descent, attaining a basin
> Ten feet wide and eighteen feet long, with whiteness and fury
> Occupied partly, but mostly pellucid, pure, a mirror;
> Beautiful there for the colour derived from green rocks under;
> Beautiful, most of all, where beads of foam uprising
> Mingle their clouds of white with the delicate hue of its
>   stillness,
> Cliff over cliff for its sides, with rowan and pendent birch
>   boughs;
> Here it lies unthought of above at the bridge and the pathway,
> Still more enclosed from below by wood and rocky projection."

Now I take leave to say that this is not poetry at all; and,
further, that if it had appeared in a three volume novel in prose—
and it might easily be printed in a prose guise without a reader
suspecting it to be anything else—it would never have occurred to
any human being to make a remark about it, unless it were to
observe that it is rather jerky.

sistence imposed upon the unreflecting crowd
the exaggerated estimate of Mr. Tennyson
against which I have protested, are now striving
to induce them to abandon their idol and set up
another. Where they have long put Mr. Tennyson, they now want to place Mr. Browning. I
propose to deal with the reasons which can be
adduced in support of this new opinion; but,
before entering on the task, I wish to point out
what this change of opinion, whether it be sound
or unsound, really signifies. It signifies that,
whether Mr. Browning be our great living poet
or not, Mr. Tennyson is confessedly ceasing to
be esteemed such by the very persons who so
noisily exalted him into that false position.
Their defection, therefore, is fatal to him, for
men never desert a true divinity when they have
once found him. They change their idols, not
their gods; and the metamorphosis of regard
which we are now witnessing, however it bears
on the fetish newly adopted, is conclusive against
the fetish newly cast aside. It is not I alone
who doubt if Mr. Tennyson be a great poet.
His quondam flatterers do the same. I deny it
explicitly. They deny it implicitly. That is the
whole difference—a difference I am quite content

to leave in that condition. What they now assert is that Mr. Browning is our great modern seer. To this, the most astounding and ludicrous pretension ever put forward in literature, let us betake ourselves.

In the year 1835, Mr. Browning, whose name at least is now sufficiently notorious, but who both then and for many years afterwards was utterly unknown to fame, wrote "Paracelsus." There was a fine opening for a poet. Byron, Shelley, Keats, Coleridge, Scott, were gone; and Wordsworth, besides being sixty-five years of age, and therefore superannuated as far as the faculty of imagination is concerned, abstained from publication. Two little volumes of verse had appeared, one in 1830, another in 1832; and the latter, containing "The Miller's Daughter," "New Year's Eve," "Lady Clara Vere de Vere," and "The Dream of Fair Women," had attracted a certain amount of attention. People spoke of their author as a poet, and justly; but it had not yet occurred to anybody to associate either his name or his work with greatness. They were waiting for the appearance of a star of larger magnitude before using up that valuable epithet. It certainly did not strike them that the author of "Paracelsus" was that star; and it would have been strange if it had. Indeed "Paracelsus" did not strike them at all. It was not a poem, whatever the writer meant it for, and the public did not mistake it for a poem. A composition in verse, however, is virtually nothing if it be not a poem; and accordingly "Paracelsus" was treated as an absolute nullity. But it was something, for all that. I do not mean to say that the public was not right in taking no notice of it. The public was quite right, and is quite right in taking no real notice of it still, though it is duly paraded in Mr. Browning's collected "Poetical Works." The absurdity lies with those who, ignoring it altogether at the time of its first appearance, would fain treat it, more than thirty years after that event, as overlooked poetry. Still, as I say, it was something, and was deserving of notice by those—necessarily, and desirably, a few—who are interested in mental peculiarities and psychical phenomena. "Paracelsus," whatever its faults, was full of thought; not poetical thought, but thought of its kind. Its thoughts were not altogether, if at all new, at least to anybody acquainted with the writings of Saint Simon and his disciples; but they were new to verse, and the individual who propounded them in that form, despite much obscurity of thought and expression, evidently possessed no ordinary powers of language. I will make but one brief quotation, which is amply sufficient for my purpose, whilst at the same time it gives a fair idea of the best passage in the whole work :—

> " Progress is
> The law of life; man's self is not yet Man !
> Nor shall I deem his object served, his end
> Attained, his genuine strength put fairly forth,
> While only here and there a star dispels
> The darkness, here and there a towering mind
> O'erlooks its prostrate fellows : when the host
> Is out at once to the despair of night,
> When all mankind alike is perfected,
> Equal in full-blown powers—then, not till then,
> I say begins man's general infancy !"

No unreflecting or uncultivated mind could write that even now ; much less could an unreflecting or uncultivated mind have written it in 1835. With the exception of the figure about a host of stars being out " to the despair of night"—which is, poetically speaking, abominably bad—there is nothing in the passage with any pretension to be poetical at all. But it is instinct with philosophical forecast (whether true or false is at present foreign to my purpose). Indeed Mr. Browning has always been well to the front in the prevailing tone of thought; and here he is strikingly distinguished from Mr. Tennyson, who is, so to speak, half-way in it and in its middle ranks. Some years later we find Mr. Tennyson introducing the selfsame views into his compositions; but by that time numbers of thoughtful Englishmen had also embraced them. But greatly as Mr. Tennyson is the inferior of Mr. Browning in catching early glimpses of philosophic truth, or what for a time is supposed to be such, he is immeasurably his superior in assimilating them into poetry. Mr. Browning not having a poetical organization, but rather a philosophical one, cannot, in his assumed *rôle* of poet, assimilate into verse these fresh scientific theories. All that his mechanical Muse can do with them is to churn and muddle them, and the result is that we should infinitely prefer to have them from Mr. Browning as Mr. Browning himself first received them—in prose.

And here we arrive at a most important observation. It is often said that no person can speak a language well until he can think in it. The remark is still more applicable to poetry. A man, to write poetry, must think in poetry. Thinking in prose, and then turning that prose thought into metre, will not do. Verse, no doubt—and perhaps very good verse—will be the result, but not poetry; at the very best only a plausible simulation of it. That Mr. Tennyson often, if indeed not usually, thinks in poetry what he writes in verse, ·nobody can doubt. The thought comes to him poetically, and he renders it poetically. Now, Mr. Browning rarely, if ever, thinks in poetry. His thoughts are often tremendously deep thoughts—deeper than any Mr. Tennyson is ever visited by ; but they reach him in the guise of prose, and, so reaching him, quit him in substantially the same form, though draped on their reappearance in the disguise of verse.

Let me very briefly illustrate my meaning. Southey, as is well known, kept a Commonplace Book in which he habitually jotted down various thoughts and observations, some of which he intended later, when he had time, to turn into what he thought poetry, but what most people are now agreed is nothing of the kind. Wordsworth also kept tablets, in his brain at least, with the same object. The result is—and as my estimate of his poetical powers is so high and has already been so strongly expressed, I have the less hesitation in saying it—that fully one-half of what Wordsworth too has written, is hardly anything more than verse. But when he is not referring to his mental tablets, but is yielding to the urgent passion of the moment, how he rises into true unmistakable poetry ! Unintentionally, no doubt—for he thereby utterly upsets his own theorising on the subject elsewhere—he lets us see in some of his most poetical passages the very process by which they were arrived at :—

> " A herdsman on the lonely mountain tops,
>   Such intercourse was his, and in this sort
>   Was his existence oftentimes *possessed.*"

Mark the significance of that word " possessed." He goes on to describe how the herdsman "in the mountains did *feel* his faith ;" how he lay "on the green turf in pensive idleness ;" how

> "Nature was at his heart as if he *felt,*
>   Though yet he knew not how, a wasting power
>   In all things which from her sweet influence
>   Might tend to wean him."

He speaks of his being " *overpowered* by Nature," and " the first virgin passion of a soul

communing with the glorious universe." If the
reader will refer to the quotations I made from
Wordsworth in the essay on Mr. Tennyson, he
will be again struck with the same thing :—

> " In such access of mind, in such high hour
>   Of visitation from the living God,
>   Thought was not; in enjoyment it expired."

He goes, you see, so far as to say that
"thought was not." He was not thinking at
all; certainly he was not referring to his tablets
or jotting down fresh memoranda. He was being
visited by the living God. God was thinking
for him, pouring divine thoughts through him ;
him who had—as all great poets, and great poets
only, have—channels ready-made for the reception
and transmission of such precious messages.

Turn we now again to Mr. Browning, whom
I have been bearing well in mind during what
may perhaps have seemed a digression, but what
has the closest relevancy to his case. Whether
Mr. Browning keeps a Commonplace Book, we
have no means of knowing; but we have every
means of knowing that he thinks in prose, for the
prose thoughts are there before us, gratuitously
turned by some arbitrary whim, which I confess

completely puzzles me, into metre. Mr. Browning is, as I have said, a profound thinker, and nearly all his thoughts have the quality of depth. Now, probably all thoughts to which this quality of depth can be ascribed, arrive at the portals of the brain in prose—their natural vesture; whilst, on the contrary, lofty thoughts, their antitheses, usually enter it in the subtle garb of music. Here we have a clear difference in kind; prose thoughts, so to speak, from below—poetical thoughts, so to speak, from above. If we suppose a permeable plane dividing these two regions of thought, we can easily understand how there comes to be what we may call a sliding scale of poets, and a sliding scale of philosophical thinkers; some of the latter, to whom the faculty of philosophising cannot be denied, being rather shallow —some of the former, whose claims to poetical status cannot fairly be questioned, not being very soaring; and we can further understand how the natural denizens of one sphere may ever and anon cross the permeable plane, invade the other sphere, and seem to belong to it in the sense in which foreigners belong to a country they are constantly visiting. But for all that there ever remains a substantial difference between the two

spheres and between their respective native in-
habitants, between the country of poetry and the
country of prose, between poetical power and
instinct and philosophical power and proclivity.
Accordingly, where a man talks the language of
the sphere to which he properly belongs—in
other words, when the philosophical thinker pub-
lishes his thoughts in prose, or a poetical thinker
addresses us in verse—our task is comparatively
simple.   All we have got to do is to decide
whether the former be profound or shallow, and
whether the latter have a lofty or a lagging
pinion.   It is when a man affects to talk the
language of the sphere to which he does not
essentially belong, that he deceives some people,
and puzzles us all.   This is precisely what Mr.
Browning has done.   Hence most people scarcely
know what to make of this poetico-philosophical
hybrid, this claimant to the great inheritance of
bardic fame, whose hands are the hands of Esau,
but whose voice is the voice of Jacob.   Several,
whose eyes, like those of Isaac, are dim, and
who therefore cannot see, admit the claim—hesi-
tatingly, it is true, again like Isaac—of the hands,
and accept him as a poet.   But it is the true
resonant voice, not the made-up delusive hand,

which is the test of the singer; and to those
whose sight is not dim, Mr. Browning is not a
poet at all—save in the sense that all cultivated
men and women of sensitive feelings are poets—
but a deep thinker, a profound philosopher, a
keen analyser, and a biting wit. With this key
to what to most persons is a riddle—for, despite
the importunate attempts of certain critics who,
as I have already said, having placed Mr.
Tennyson on a poetical pedestal considerably
too high for him, are now beginning to waver in
their extravagant creed, and are disposed to put
him on one a trifle lower, placing Mr. Browning
there instead, the general public has not yet
become quite reconciled to the operation—I think
I shall be able to rid them of their perplexities.
At any rate, I will keep applying it as we go
along.

Let us revert to " Paracelsus," and take our
start from it, as Mr. Browning himself did. His
lyrical pieces apart—of which something anon—
and the humouristic faculty which has since
developed itself in him, Mr. Browning in " Paracelsus," is what Mr. Browning is in all the many
so-called poetical works he has since given to the
world. He is Mr. Browning, naturally not yet

grown to his full size; not yet quite so deep, shrewd, obscure, fantastical, unmusical; but with the exceptions we have just made, what manner, and matter of mental man he is may there be satisfactorily scrutinized. He is at his never-abandoned natural task of thinking deep thoughts in prose, and his artificial trick of turning them into verse. He is, as he imagines, working like a dramatist, just as he has since imagined himself to be working as a dramatist in such pieces as " Bishop Blougram's Apology," " Caliban on Setebos," etc. Indeed, he has let us into the secret of his method in " Sordello," written very shortly after " Paracelsus," in the following lines; which I quote, though at the risk perhaps of most of my readers declaring that they have not the faintest notion as to what they mean:

<blockquote>

" How I rose,
And how you have advanced! since evermore
Yourselves effect what I was fain before
Effect, what I supplied yourselves suggest,
What I leave bare yourselves can now invest.
How we attain to talk as brothers talk,
In half-words, call things by half-names, no balk
From discontinuing old aids. To-day
Takes in account the work of Yesterday:
Has not the world a Past now, its adept
</blockquote>

New aids?   A single touch more may enhance,
A touch less turn to insignificance,
Those structures' symmetry the Past has strewed
The world with, once so bare.   Leave the mere rude
Explicit details ! 'tis but brother's speech
We need, speech where an accent's change gives each
The other's soul—no speech to understand
By former audience : need was then to expand,
Expatiate—hardly were we brothers ! true—
Nor I lament my small remove from you,
Nor reconstruct what stands already.   Ends
Accomplished turn to means : my art intends
New structure from the ancient."

It must not be supposed that I quote this
passage with approbation.   Not only do I think
it not poetry, but I think it detestable gibberish,
even if I look at it as prose.   Had Mr. Browning
been writing *bonâ fide* prose, he would have put
it very differently and much more intelligibly ;
but talking, to revert to our metaphor, in a
foreign language over which he has not obtained
due mastery, he is shockingly unintelligible, or
at least painfully difficult to understand.   By
dint of great trouble I have arrived at understanding the above passage, and will endeavour
briefly to explain its meaning.   The reader has
no doubt heard the vulgar proverb, " A nod is as
good as a wink to a blind horse."   Mr. Browning

wishes to intimate that a nod or a wink is really and seriously as good to an intelligent man of the nineteenth century as formal speech. Shakespeare, and such unfortunate individuals, having had to deal with an inferior set of people, were compelled to use "rude explicit details." Mr. Browning's "art intending new structure from the ancient," has only to "talk in half-words, call things by half-names," and if they do not understand him, the fault is theirs of course, not his. They are not his brothers. In this same "Sordello," from which I am quoting, over each page stands a prose heading, which is a continuation of the foregoing one. Over the passage from which I have made the above extract, the following headings occur : "He asserts the poet's rank and right, Basing these on their proper ground, Recognizing true dignity in service, Whether successively that of Epoist, *Dramatist, or, so to call him, analyst,* Who turns in due course synthesist."

Now the last two headings are of great importance, just as is the passage in verse below them which I have quoted, because, however false may be their matter, and however deplorable their manner, they contain Mr. Browning's own estimate of his office, and his own account of his method. As such, they are invaluable to us. Just one more brief confession on his part will complete for us the idea, as understood by himself, of his functions as a poet. In the Dedication of "Sordello" to Mr. Milsand, written in 1863, or twenty-three years after it was first published, Mr. Browning writes : "The historical decoration was purposely of no more importance than a background requires ; and my stress lay on the incidents in the development of a soul: *little else is worth study. I, at least, always thought so.*" Thus Mr. Browning's office, according to his own account, is that of an analyst who turns in due course synthesist and developes a soul by half-words; or, as I should put it, it is to get inside an imaginary or historical personage, and evolve him for the benefit of the intelligent public by nods and winks. This is how his "new art intends new structure from the ancient."

I hope my readers understand me ; for, if they do not, they will certainly never understand Mr. Browning, and it is highly desirable that they should understand so much of him as the foregoing, both in order to be able to measure

him as he asks to be measured, and to appreciate
this account of him, which a very little reflection
will show to be in perfect harmony with, and indeed substantially the same as, his own account
of himself.   What is his own account of himself?
An analyst who turns in due course synthesist,
whose subject matter is souls, and whose method
of communication with the outer world is half-
words arranged in metre.   What is my account
of him?   A subtle, profound, conscious psycho-
logist, who scientifically gets inside souls, and,
having scrutinized their thoughts and motives in
a prose and methodical fashion, then makes them
give the result, as if they had been scrutinizing
themselves, in verse.   This latter operation Mr.
Browning evidently imagines is synthesis.   There
never was a more ludicrous mistake.   It is, in
reality, nothing more than the analysis completed
and stated, and is no more synthesis than a
lecture by Professor Huxley on the *vertebrata* is
an animal.   Mr. Browning labours under the
greatest possible delusion when he imagines that
he ever "turns in due course synthesist."   That
is precisely what he never does.   He remains a
mere analyst to the end of the chapter, pottering
about among the brains and entrails of the souls

he has dissected, and utterly unable to do anything with them, except to call attention to the component parts he has skilfully laid bare with his knife. It would be wonderful if he could do anything more; just as wonderful as it would be if the anatomical professor could put together again the poor carcass of the dog he has reduced to so many inanimate members. He can galvanise them, it is true, for a moment, into simulating life. So can Mr. Browning. But that is the range of the synthesis of both of them. If Mr. Browning wants to know of a dramatist who is a real synthesist, I can easily tell him of one. His name is Shakespeare. But, then, Shakespeare was, luckily, not so great in analysis as Mr. Browning. Speaking properly, Shakespeare never analyses at all in our presence, and probably never did so even in the presence of his own consciousness, any more than millions of men, who speak grammatically, analyse the construction of their sentences before they utter them. Every real drama—indeed every real work of plastic (as opposed to mere technic) art —is an organism, a growth, a vitality, just as much as is a bird, a tree, or a mammal. Not only is it true that a poet is born, not made, but

it is equally true that his poem is born, not
made.* In his brain, heart, soul, whatever we
like to call it—in his being would be, perhaps,
the best word—exists the seed or germ of a
poem or of many poems ; and all that external
conditions, sights, sounds, experiences, can do
for this seed or germ is to foster or to check it.
But the thing itself, the real living, poetic pro-
toplasm, is not to be had or got *ab extra.* Going
about seizing upon objects and submitting them
to analysis, even though synthesis be then superadded, will by no means produce poetry, or any
work of plastic art—using the word art properly,
as opposed to craft. Otherwise a chemist, who
finds out what a particular kind of gunpowder is
made of, and then makes it, would be a poet.
For to him is peculiarly applicable Mr. Browning's definition of " dramatist"—terrible dramatist indeed ! " or, so to speak, analyst, who turns
in due course synthesist." But there is an im-
passable difference between dramas and deto-
nating powder, and also between the processes

* Hence the difficulty of defining poetry, just as there exists
the well-known difficulty of defining life. But just as despite the
latter difficulty we can always say in any particular instance what
is *not* life, so despite the former one we can say in any particular
instance what is not poetry.

by which they are to be produced. I freely grant —indeed, I more than grant, I insist—that Mr. Browning, whatever may be said against his synthetical powers (and, as we have seen, even if he had them to perfection, he would not necessarily be a poet), is great as an analyst. But the analysed goose of the fable laid no more golden eggs; and analysed souls are just as little likely ever again to speak golden words. It is not the province of the poet to perform any such operation. It is the province of such men as Hartley, James Mill, and Professor Bain, and admirably do they perform their work. But we have not got any poems from them, nor is it likely that from the only living one of the illustrious trio we ever shall. Having a distinct comprehension of their office and its limits, they have accordingly kept within the sphere—the sphere of deep prose thoughts as opposed to that of lofty poetical thoughts, of which we have spoken—to which their talents and task naturally belonged. Hence their labours have been of inestimable service to the world. But Mr. Browning has perversely flitted from one sphere to the other, insisted on making himself at home where he is a perfect stranger, uttered profound thoughts in would-be poetic idiom, an idiom foreign to them and to him, and involved them accordingly in such abominable jargon that, when he and his affected admirers have passed away, they will be utterly lost to the world—for they *will* be a loss, on account of their depth—and buried in permanent oblivion. Should he possibly be remembered at all, it will be because posterity, condensing this our judgment, will inscribe on his grave the words of Martial:

> " Carmina . . . . scribis et Apolline nullo
> Laudari debes."

Anglicè:

> " You kept on twanging at your lyre,
> Though no Apollo did inspire."

So much for Mr. Browning's *novum organum,* or new method of making poetry. Having considered the subject-matter of his work, and the process by which he labours on it, we have now only to examine the form in which he presents it, when finished, to the public gaze. In other words, having scrutinized his matter and method, we have now to look at his manner, or, to speak still more plainly, his expression—those " half-words," as he has himself called them, whereby he communicates with intelligent readers. Now, why does Mr. Browning communicate his thoughts in this fashion of half-words? The answer is exceedingly simple. Because, if he communicated them in full ones—*i.e.*, explicitly and clearly—though still in verse, their prose nature would be seen at a glance by everybody; and everybody, the simplest person as well as the most pedantic, could not fail to perceive that the author was whimsically and gratuitously measuring them out into certain lengths, instead of unaffectedly not caring how many metrical feet there were in them, or whether they formed feet at all. For there is no difficulty in putting anything into verse, as may be seen in the versified rules of the "Gradus ad Parnassum," or in the advertisements of Mr. Moses, the cheap outfitter. It would require very little ingenuity to turn "Euclid" into metre, and, for anything I know, it may already have been done. But, as in these instances the primary object is to be understood, the reader sees at once that he is not reading, or supposed to be reading, poetry, but only metre, so employed for mnemonic or for catchpenny purposes. In Mr. Browning's case the unsophisticated reader really does not know what it is he is reading. It is printed in arbitrary lengths, and therefore looks as if it cannot well be prose; yet it does not, as a rule, read like verse, and in nearly all cases its meaning is obscure, and in none very obvious. If it were, Mr. Browning would be found out without more ado. I do not mean to say that he consciously deceives his readers; he deceives his readers and himself too. He is the real M. Jourdain, who has been writing prose all his life without knowing it; very bad prose, it is true, as half-words arranged in lengths necessarily must be, but prose all the same. It would be idle to quote instances of this, for his works are one long almost uninterrupted instance of it. You may open any one of his volumes at any page you like for proof of the assertion. Surely the two passages I have already quoted from him, though for a totally different purpose, will suffice as instances. If

> " Since evermore
> Yourselves effect what I was fain before
> Effect, what I supplied yourselves suggest,
> What I leave bare yourselves can now invest"

does not strike everybody as very bad prose, consisting of half-words arranged in lengths, I

own myself fairly beaten, or at least baffled in
my demonstration. And what is true of these
passages is true of Mr. Browning's compositions
passim. For poetic thought has its natural
utterance or expression, just as everything else
has, and you cannot make it express itself differently save by travestying it. To put the case as
extremely as possible, yet without travelling one
hair's breadth beyond the limits of the strictest
truth, a living tree expresses itself in foliage not
more necessarily than does poetic thought express itself in a certain and inevitable kind and
form of diction. But what is the diction of
poetry ? Is it half-words arranged in lengths ?
Is it obscure diction of any sort ? Is the diction
of poetry anything but diction that is at once
clear—*that,* it shares with other diction—lofty,
and musical ? Who are the clearest and most
musical poets ? Unquestionably the great poets.
Whose blank verse is fit to be mentioned, even
for mere sound, after Shakespeare's ? Only
Milton's; and his, *longo intervallo.* Mr. Tennyson's, smooth as it is, is the poorest stuff compared with the blank verse of Shakespeare or
Milton. It is melodious enough, no doubt (just
as Moore, in rhyme, is the perfection of melody);

but where is its harmony—where are the infinite harmonies in it? They are wanting. For melody is not the only thing in music. All the wonderful combinations that come of an innate familiarity with the use of fugue and counterpoint make something very different from mere melody. Shakespeare and Milton betray this innate familiarity in blank verse; Spenser and Byron betray it in rhyme; and so, whilst they are the greatest of our poets in other respects, they are, when one once knows what music really means and is, the most musical. Similarly they are the most clear. Poor Mr. Browning is both muddy and unmusical to the last degree. In fact, his style may fairly be described as the very incarnation of discordant obscurity. Is it wonderful? He has no voice, and yet he wants to sing. He is not a poet, and yet he would fain write poetry. We have no right to be surprised if he is inarticulate, and if we get only half-words cut into lengths. The wonder would be if we got anything else. In reading Mr. Browning, we are perpetually reminded of those lines in Mr. Bailey's " Festus " :

<blockquote>
" The dress of words,
Like to the Roman girl's enticing garb,
</blockquote>

> Should let the play of limb be seen through it.
> . . . . *A mist of words,*
> *Like halos round the moon, though they enlarge*
> *The seeming size of thoughts, make the light less.*"

But, it will be urged, there is occasionally something else in Mr. Browning, which, if not poetry, is at least something very like poetry. Exactly: there is. But when? When Mr. Browning ceases to be Mr. Browning proper, when his *differentia* disappears, and he is no longer Mr. Browning "the dramatist, or, so to call him, analyst," but Mr. Browning the man pure and simple. It will be remembered that I have already incidentally said that Mr. Browning is not a poet save in the sense that all cultivated men and women of sensitive feelings are poets ; and the statement was made deliberately, and with the intention of reverting to it here. It would therefore be strange indeed if in the course of thirty-five years' obstinate practice of writing verse Mr. Browning had not once or twice deviated into penning something that resembled poetry, and was so much on the border-land of poetry or even across it, that it ought to bear that name. Be it so. All that I am arguing for is that Mr. Browning is not specifically a poet, but is specifically something quite different.   The poetic temperament and intellect are not the *proprium* of Mr. Browning, but only the *accidens.*   But let us see what is the highest result, when the latter has, so to speak, the upper hand, or the command of him.

> " Oh ! to be in England
> Now that April's there ;
> And whosoever wakes in England
> Sees, some morning, unaware,
> That the lowest boughs and the brush-wood sheaf
> Round the elm-tree bole are in tiny leaf,
> While the chaffinch sings on the orchard bough
> In England—now ! "
>
> *Lyrics.*

> " Love like mine must have return,
> I thought : no river starts but to some sea."
>
> *A Soul's Tragedy.*

Is this poetry ?   If it is, it is of a very commonplace sort, rather above than below average Magazine verse, and many examples of it from Mr. Browning could be produced, inasmuch as he perpetually, indeed invariably, lapses into commonplace when he allows himself to think, on the poetic side, naturally.   Often, as though conscious that what poetic utterance he has in common with ordinarily cultivated men and

women of sensitive feelings is of this com-
plexion, he will not allow himself to think
naturally, but strains at being original whilst
still wanting to remain poetical. Then the result is lamentable; is⁀ in fact, spasmodic. For
instance :

> " Earth is a wintry clod :
> But spring-wind, like a dancing psaltress, passes
> Over its breast to waken it." *Paracelsus.*

> ' The sprinkled isles,
> Lily on lily, that o'erlace the sea,
> And laugh their pride when the light wave lisps,
> ' Greece.' " *Cleon.*

> " One wave,
> Feeling the foot of Him upon its neck,
> Gaped as a snake does, lolled out its large tongue,
> And licked the whole labour flat."
> *Dramatis Personæ.*

> " Is it better in May? I ask you. You've summer all at
> once;
> In a day he leaps complete with a few strong April
> suns !
> 'Mid the sharp short emerald wheat, scarce risen three
> fingers well,
> The wild tulip, at end of its tube, blows out its great
> red bell,
> Like a thin clear bubble of blood, for the children to
> pick and sell."
> *Up at a Villa—Down in the City.*

These are pure spasms; specimens of the mental action of a man who is striving earnestly to be an original poet, and who for the life of him cannot be—since no striving will make a man such, any more than it will give him wings. Mr. John Stuart Mill has in one of his admirable "Dissertations and Discussions" made the unfortunate remark that probably any man of good abilities might, by determination and persistence, end by becoming as great a poet as Wordsworth —he himself thinking very highly of Wordsworth as a poet. In any philosophical question I should differ from Mr. Mill with great diffidence; but I have not a moment's hesitation in saying that such an assertion, save as applied to—say—one-half of Wordsworth's compositions, which, as I have already remarked, are perhaps not poetry at all, but only verse, must be described, despite the reverence I feel for Mr. Mill, as fundamentally erroneous. Accepted, however, to the limited extent I have prescribed to it, the assertion is true enough, and it is singularly applicable to Mr. Browning. Any ordinarily cultivated person of sensitive feelings who could write verse might have written the first two commonplace passages just quoted from Mr. Browning, and, being resolved to be original, might have strained himself till he concocted the last four. The former are examples of such natural versified speech as might be attained by almost anybody. The latter are instances of that artificial, acquired, laborious, *foreign* speech which is necessarily fallen into by people who are clumsily translating complex thoughts into an alien tongue. As for such pieces as " Marching Along," and " How they Brought the Good News from Ghent," they cannot be classed, at the very highest estimate, save with Macaulay's " Lays of Rome," to which surely no impartial person can doubt they are very inferior—and yet no one talks or thinks of Macaulay as specifically a poet—and ought more fairly to be classed with the Cavalier Songs of Mr. Walter Thornbury, whom no one has ever dreamt of alluding to save as a very spirited versifier.

Thus, as far as we have inquired, we find Mr. Browning in his attempted *rôle* of poet, to be doing three things, and generally the first of them. Either playing the part of analyist, getting inside souls, and developing them to the reader by half-words, which is not writing poetry at all ; or writing simple intelligible verse, which, if it is to be considered poetry, must honestly be described as commonplace poetry, both easy and by no means infrequent of production; or, in dread and dislike of being commonplace, writing what has happily been termed spasmodic poetry, poetry that comes of violent straining after effect, and which ought, on no account, to be written by anybody, since it sins against that eternal truth, so well put in the same passage in " Festus " from which I have already quoted:

> " Simplicity
> Is nature's first step, and the last of art."

Which quotation I may supplement, for the benefit of Mr. Browning and his admirers, by another from a still higher authority, and in itself still more suggestive and instructive:

> " This is an art
> Which doth mend nature, change it rather, but
> The art itself is nature."
>
> *Winter's Tale*, iv. 3.

That is just the art which Mr. Browning has not got.

But how about " Andrea del Sarto," " Fra Lippo Lippi," " A Death in the Desert," " Caliban on Setebos," and " Bishop Blougram's Apology ?" What have I to say about these? This much. That, with the exception of " Caliban on Setebos "—which, on account of its rendering certain prevailing modes of thought on theological questions, has been very much over-estimated—they are productions betraying the possession of peculiar imagination, of mordant wit of almost the highest kind, of a delicious sense of humour, and, in " Andrea del Sarto," of deep tenderness. But neither tenderness, nor humour, nor wit, nor even imagination, nor indeed all these together, will constitute a man a poet. Laplace, Bacon,* Copernicus, Newton, Mr. Darwin—all have immense imagination ; and the list might, of course, be extended·indefinitely. I think I have allowed it to be seen that I regard Mr. Browning's intellectual powers as very considerable indeed. " Bishop Blougram's Apology "

* A brief extract from Mr. Bain upon the nature of Bacon's genius will throw some light on this subject. " Although Bacon's imagery," says that profound and accurate writer, " sometimes rises to poetry, this is not its usual character; his was not a poetic sense of Nature, but a broad general susceptibility, partaking more of the natural historian than of the poet, by which all the objects coming before his view or presented to his imagination took a deep hold, and, by the help of his intense attraction of similarity, were recalled on the slightest similitude. Many great writers in English literature have had this strong susceptibility to the sensible world at large without a special poetic sense, while some have had the poetic sense superadded. These last are our greatest poets." This is nearly as good an account of Mr. Browning's " sense of Nature " as it is of Bacon's.

is an astonishing production, which one invariably reads almost throughout with unflagging zest. But it is not poetry. There is not a line of poetry in it from first to last. Suppose he had never written anything else, would it have occurred to anybody that he was a poet, or even aspiring to be a poet ?

In order still further to illustrate our meaning, suppose Mr. Tennyson had never written anything but "The Northern Farmer"—a piece one chuckles over with inexpressible delight—again, would it have occurred to anybody that Mr. Tennyson was a poet, or was pretending to be such ? Of course not; no more than it would have occurred to his contemporaries to have regarded Cowper as a poet if he had never written anything but "John Gilpin," whose pre-eminent success positively annoyed its author ? So with "Bishop Blougram's Apology," and all of Mr. Browning's compositions, or passages in his compositions, which are *ejusdem generis* with it. They are witty, wise, shrewd, deep, true, wonderful—anything or everything but poetry. It is the greatest, though apparently the commonest, mistake in the world to suppose that the quality of verse, provided the thoughts it expresses are excellent thoughts, involves for those thoughts and their expression the quality of poetry. This has been Mr. Browning's *ignis fatuus* through life; and the absurd chase it has led him he in turn has led those who have not found out what it is he has all along been following. In a word, Mr. Browning's so-called Muse is a *lusus naturæ*, a sport, to use gardeners' language; but certain sapient critics have been exulting over it, as though it were a new and finer specimen of the old true poetic stock. Moreover, Mr. Browning's undoubted faculty of depth has bewitched and bewrayed them. Despite their protestations of being perfectly content with Mr. Tennyson as the great poet who justifies the period, they are not content with him. They have all along more or less consciously felt what I insisted on in the last essay—his want of loftiness. Now, in Mr. Browning they have found something that unquestionably is not in Mr. Tennyson, and they have begun to fancy that that something may possibly supply Mr. Tennyson's shortcomings. That comes of not having thought the matter out with regard to either of these authors.* They know Mr.

---

* To illustrate the lax nonsense that is written on this subject, take the following propositions from the " Spectator :"—" Mr.

Tennyson wants something or other; they know Mr. Browning has something or other. But from lack of patient reflection and investigation they fail to perceive for themselves that what Mr. Tennyson wants is height, and what Mr. Browning has is depth. This once clearly perceived, it is obvious that the latter characteristic cannot mend the imperfection of the former characteristic. You might just as well try to make a mountain higher by excavating round it, or make swallows fly more soaringly by yourself descending a coal-pit. My estimate of Mr. Tennyson as a poet has been already very explicitly given; and though it is such as thousands

Browning would perhaps make a great dramatist," using the word dramatist in the sense of writer for the stage. The critic who hazards such an assertion can either know nothing really of Mr. Browning or nothing of the very elements of dramatic representation. Again: "Though not the widest, the most powerful, or the freest, we hold Tennyson the deepest, by far (Clough perhaps excepted, above whom, of course, in almost all other respects he must rank), of all English poets after Shakespeare, and superior to Byron in every characteristic of a poet, except one of the greater characteristics, fire." The only epithet that properly describes this sentence, which mainly consists of a series of clashing indefinite adjectives, is muddle-speeched. The writer, who signs himself "Ed. Spectator," obviously does not even know what he himself thinks on the subject. In other words, he has never thought the matter out. Why will the "Spectator" persist in always serving up its thoughts *raw?*

of men who have fancied themselves beloved of
the Muses would leap with joy to have honestly
formed of them, it is far removed from that in
which his more ardent admirers at .times affect to
indulge. One thing, however, is certain. They
need be in no fear lest Mr. Tennyson should be
displaced by any critic in his sound senses to
make way for Mr. Browning. When men desire
to behold the flight of an eagle, and cannot get
it, they do not usually regard the tramp of an
elephant as a substitute.

I would therefore beg of the general public
to return to the bent of its own original judgment,
and unbewildered by those who would fain be
its guides, to treat Mr. Browning's " Poetical
Works" as it treated " Paracelsus," etc., on its
first appearance—as though they were non-
existent. I know it has now much to contend
against. When the academy and the drawing-
room, when pedantry and folly, combine to set
a fashion, it requires more self-confidence than
the meek public commonly possesses to laugh
the silly innovation down. To Mr. Tennyson's
credit be it spoken, he has never gone looking
for fame. The ground we tread on is delicate ;
and I will, therefore, only add that one should have

been better pleased if the author, who is now so ridiculously obtruded as his rival, had imitated him in that particular. Small London literary coteries, and large fashionable London salons, cannot crown a man with the bays of Apollo. They may stick their trumpery tinsel wreaths upon him, but these will last no longer than the locks they encircle. They may confer notoriety, but fame is not in their gift. All they can bestow is as transitory as themselves. Let the sane general public, therefore, I say, take heart, and bluntly forswear Mr. Browning and all his works. It is bad enough that there should be people, pretending to authority among us, who call a man a great poet when, though unquestionably a poet, he has no marks of greatness about him. But that is a venial error, and a trifling misfortune, compared to what would be the misery of living in an age which gibbeted itself beforehand for the pity of posterity, by deliberately calling a man a poet who—however remarkable his mental attributes and powers—is not specifically a poet at all. I hope we shall be spared this humiliation. At any rate, I must protest against being supposed willingly to participate in it.

Mr. Swinburne.

N my essay on Mr. Browning I have shown how dissatisfaction with the poetry of Mr. Tennyson, as an exponent of the age, has driven even his once frantic admirers to hearken for yet another voice, and how, in their ignorance of what it is in Mr. Tennyson that fails to satisfy them, they have pitched upon Mr. Browning of all people to supply the omission. What Mr. Tennyson wanted, I said, was loftiness ; what Mr. Browning possessed, I observed, was depth ; and I added that, this distinction once made, it was obvious that the one could not possibly supplement the other, having no earthly affinity with it. But there exists another distinction between them, which, though in complete harmony with the one I have already drawn, sets the

matter in another, and for my present purpose still more important, light. If I were asked to sum up the characteristics of Mr. Tennyson's compositions in a single word, the word I should employ would be " feminine," and if I had to do the same for Mr. Browning's genius, the word inevitably selected would be " studious." The pen of the latter is essentially the pen of a student ; the muse of the former is essentially— I must not say the muse of a woman, for I should be rendering myself liable to misconception, but —a feminine muse. And in these two salient qualities they are unquestionably representative men, and typify two of the prominent tendencies of the time. We have just had, from a much revered source, an essay on the Subjection of Women ; but I think it would not be difficult to show that men, and especially in the domain of Art, are, and have for some time been, quite as subject to women, to say the least of it, as is desirable. In the region of morals, women may, in modern times, have had a beneficent influence ; though, as we shall see when we come to treat of Mr. Swinburne's particular genius, recent pheno-mena have somewhat shaken the once favourable opinion on that score. But there can be no

question that, in the region of Art, their influence
has been unmitigatedly mischievous. They have
ruined the stage ; they have dwarfed painting till
it has become little more than the representative
of pretty little sentiment—much of it terribly false
—and mawkish commonplace domesticities ; and
they have helped poetry to become, in the hands
of Mr. Tennyson at least, and of his disciples,
the mere handmaid of their own limited interests,
susceptibilities, and yearnings. I do not say
that Mr. Tennyson is never by any chance and
on occasion fairly manly, though I think no
one can doubt who considers the matter, that
he is not even fairly manly very often, and
never conspicuously so ; and the most unreasonable of his worshippers would not dare for
one moment, in describing his supposed merits
as a poet, to call him masculine. That feminine is the proper word to apply to his compositions, taken in their ˉentirety, no impartial
judge, I feel convinced, would dream of denying.

Between the essentially feminine genius and
the genius of the student there is an abyss ; and
it represents the enormous difference that there
is between Mr. Tennyson and Mr. Browning. I

am not again going to discuss Mr. Browning's studious quality, for I have already so fully insisted on the " depth " of his genius in my last paper— and between depth and studiousness there is so obvious a similarity—that I may fairly assume the point as settled. What I now wish to note is, that whilst, as I have said, not altogether satisfied with Mr. Tennyson's feminine, unlofty way of looking at things, the critics, who are so enamoured of their age that they are determined to find in it great poetry somewhere or other, pitched upon the deep and studious Mr. Browning, in the hope that he would afford them the satisfaction they required; they have, in reality, failed, despite all their bravado and assurances to the contrary, to find it in that quarter. It was simply impossible that they should find it there. A studious writer is neither the complement nor the antithesis of a feminine one. When men say, " This poet is too feminine," what they want, of course, is a poet who shall be masculine. A student, as far as sex is concerned, as far as manly and womanly qualities are involved, is a nondescript. He may be incidentally of a masculine or of a feminine turn, just as it happens. He is a neutral in the matter. It does so happen that Mr. Browning is certainly far more masculine than feminine in his studiousness ; but his masculinity is a mere sub-quality to that one great predominating characteristic. He is, over and above all things, an Analyser, and every other attribute is merged and lost, so to speak, in its conspicuous supremacy. Little wonderful, therefore, was it that these same critics, still sadly wanting an adequate poet, for all their copious assurances that they already possessed a couple, warmly welcomed Mr. Swinburne's appearance, and, enrolling him at once with the other two, have exultingly formed for themselves a Trinity of Song. Mr. Swinburne may thank Mr. Tennyson's imperfections and Mr. Browning's shortcomings for the reception he has met with ; for let me hasten to say that, had a really great, adequate poet been alive, Mr. Swinburne would have failed to attract much attention, save for those qualities which even his admirers do not admire, but of which I may remark that I shall be found very tolerant. But the existence of Mr. Tennyson and Mr. Browning left ample room for Mr. Swinburne, just as the existence of Mr. Tennyson, Mr. Browning, and Mr. Swinburne still leaves ᴀmple room for another, or indeed many another, poetical apparition.

It might be supposed, after what has been said, that, even though Mr. Swinburne should turn out, on examination, to be neither the one great poet we should all be so delighted to hail, nor even a poet bringing precisely those qualities which neither the feminine nor the studious temperament supplies, he would at any rate have contributed something strikingly distinct from what we have seen is contributed by the other two, and be as different from Mr. Tennyson and from Mr. Browning as they are from each other. Different in every respect he unquestionably is from Mr. Browning, as every poet—and Mr. Swinburne *is* a poet—necessarily must be; Mr. Browning not being specifically a poet at all. It is with Mr. Tennyson, therefore, we must compare or contrast him; and thus, once for all, we may dismiss Mr. Browning to his own studious prose territory, having no further need of him in the poetical one.

Now, on the first blush, it would seem as though Mr. Swinburne's poetry were a genuine revolt against that of Mr. Tennyson, and as though he had struck a distinct and even antagonistic note. That Mr. Swinburne himself thinks so is evident from some observations dropped by him in his "Notes on Poems and Reviews:" a defence of his muse against the strictures of those who complained—in my opinion, with absurd extravagance—of its alleged indecency and profanity.

"In one thing," he says, "it seems I have erred: I have forgotten to prefix to my work the timely warning of a great poet and humourist :—

> "'J'en préviens les mères des familles,
> Ce que j'écris n'est pas pour les petites filles
> Dont on coupe le pain en tartines; mes vers
> Sont des vers de jeune homme.'

"I have overlooked the evidence which every day makes clear, that our time has room only for such as are content to write for children and girls. . . . . Happily, there is no fear that the supply of milk for babes will fall short of the demand for some time yet. There are moral milkmen enough, in all conscience, crying their ware about the streets and byways."

A few pages farther on Mr. Swinburne adds :—

"'The question at issue is, whether or not all

that cannot be lisped in the nursery or fingered in the school-room is therefore to be cast out of the library? whether or not the domestic circle is to be for all men and writers the outer limit and extreme horizon of their world of work? . . . Literature, to be worthy of men, must be large, liberal, sincere; and if literature is not to deal with the full life of man and the whole nature of things, let it be cast aside with the rods and rattles of childhood. Against how few really great names has not this small and dirt-encrusted pebble been thrown! A reputation seems imperfect without this tribute also; one jewel is wanting to the crown. . . . With English versifiers now, the idyllic form is alone in fashion. . . . We have idylls good and bad, ugly and pretty; idylls of the farm and the mill; idylls of the dining-room and the deanery. . . . The idyllic form is best for domestic and pastoral poetry. It is naturally on a lower level than that of tragic or lyric verse. Its gentle and maidenly lips are somewhat narrow for the stream, and somewhat cold for the fire of song. It is very fit for the sole diet of girls; not very fit for the sole sustenance of man."

The point could not be better or more clearly

put. Neither could it possibly be made more apparent that Mr. Swinburne here intends to protest against the excessive estimate usually paraded of the Laureate's poetry, both as regards its matter and its manner; and if the above is not an accusation, virtually embodying the distinction I have made, that Mr. Tennyson's muse is essentially a "feminine" one, and a trumpet-call to critics and the public to demand some more masculine stuff, and welcome it with open arms if it does appear, language must have lost all its uses. But of course it does embody such a protest against the feminine genius of Mr. Tennyson's verse, and a bold, admirably written plea for what is more "fit for the sustenance of man."

The question therefore arises, Has Mr. Swinburne, acting up to his excellent theory, turned his back on the haunts of feminine muses, struck out a masculine strain, and wrung from strenuous chords nervous and extolling hymns worthy of men and gods? Alas! who shall say it? True, he has given us no more idylls of the farm and the mill, of the dining-room and the deanery; nor will any one pretend that his lyrics and ballads are fit for the sole or even for part of the diet of girls. But what have men—to say nothing of gods—men brave, muscular, bold, upright, chivalrous—I will not say chaste, for that is scarcely a masculine quality (" I will find you twenty lascivious turtles ere one chaste man," says no less an authority than Shakespeare), but at any rate clean—men with "pride in their port, defiance in their eye," men daring, enduring, short of speech, and terrible in action —what have these to do with Mr. Swinburne's Venuses and Chastelards, his Anactorias and Faustines, his Dolores, his Sapphos, or his Hermaphroditus? If these be his Olympus, we prefer the deanery and the dining-room, or even the drawing-room. I do not say that they are not fair, much less that they are illegitimate, subjects for the poet's pen; but are they masculine? That is the question. Mr. Swinburne need fear no prudish or bigoted criticism from me. Venus or virgin, it is all one to me, provided he can make fine poetry out of either; though, of course, I should always reserve to myself the right of saying which I thought to be the nobler theme. He may take Priapus for his Apollo, if he will, so that he have dexterity and daintiness enough to handle a difficult matter becomingly, and extol a satyr into a Celestial. But it will not do to empty Olympus of its divinities, fill it with tipsy Bacchanals and meretricious Mœnads, and then conceive that idylls of the earth, earthy—idylls of the farm and the mill—have been gloriously surpassed. Is this all that his Hellenic culture has taught him? Were "Kisses that burn and bite" the everlasting theme of Homer, of Pindar, or of the grand tragedians of their country? Who was it but an Athenian that declared that poetry should consist of nothing but hymns to the gods and praises of virtue, and in the severity of his wrath at lascivious strains and Lydian measures banished all bards from his ideal republic? We hear much of the puritanical spirit of Christianity; and in non-Catholic countries there has been at times considerably too much of this. But what about the occasional puritanism of Greek paganism? It too could revolt against literary excesses, and prove that in that respect, as in many another, it can compete with the creeds that helped to overthrow it. If ever there was a thorough Christian poet, Wordsworth was surely that man. Yet so little did he associate paganism with what he, at least, would have deemed profane and indecent, that, in his despair at the temper of his own times, he cried out :—

> " Great God ! I'd rather be
> A pagan suckled in a creed outworn
> So might I, standing on this pleasant lea,
> Have glimpses that would make me less forlorn;
> Have sight of Proteus rising from the sea,
> Or hear old Triton blow his wreathëd horn."

If Mr. Swinburne be really anxious to see the fulfilment of his prophecy in his " Hymn to Proserpine"—

> " Though before thee the throned Cytherean be fallen, and hidden her head,
> Yet thy kingdom shall pass, Galilean; thy dead shall go down to thee dead "—

it were surely desirable that he did not travesty the men and women, the gods and goddesses, of that earlier time. And in what way does he travesty them? By eliminating all that was masculine—and what a masculine epoch it was !—and intensifying and exaggerating what was not masculine by aid of his modern feminine lens. For to this clear charge and distinct conclusion must we come : that far from Mr. Swinburne being more masculine even than Mr. Tennyson, he is positively less so. Where has he given us,

to use his own words, " Literature worthy of
men, large, liberal, sincere ?" Where the "literature that deals with the full life of man and the
whole nature of things?" I may readily grant
that the " lilies and languors of virtue " do not
constitute the full life of man and the whole
nature of things ; but I must protest that neither
do "the roses and raptures of vice." Is that
the sense in which he reads the magnificent
saying of Schiller, when drenched and suffused
with the old classical temper he exclaimed, " Man
has lost his dignity, but Art has saved it. Truth
still lives in fiction, and from the copy will the
original be restored." What does Mr. Swinburne
think is either the copy or the original of man's
dignity? Is it represented in such lines as
these ?—

> " Ah that my lips were tuneless lips, but pressed
> To the bruised blossom of thy scourged white breast!
> Ah that my mouth for Muses' milk were fed
> On the sweet blood thy sweet small wounds had bled!
> That with my tongue I felt them, and could taste
> The faint flakes from thy bosom to thy waist!"

I do not shrink from quoting anything Mr.
Swinburne has written, and treating it with becoming critical fairness ; but in quoting the above

lines, I should like to know if their author thinks he is using Art to save something man has lost or would otherwise lose? Is this the verse that is peculiarly "fit for the sole sustenance of man?" Mr. Tennyson, of whose extreme moral propriety some people have made such an absurd parade, has written something very similar, to the full as impassioned, and considerably better balanced:—

> "My whole soul waiting silently,
> All naked in a sultry sky,
> Droops blinded with his piercing eye:
> I *will* possess him, or will die.
> I will grow round him in his place;
> Grow, live, die looking on his face;
> Die, dying clasp'd in his embrace."

Fatima.

I distinctly remember lending the volume containing this poem to a young lady, and having it returned by her mamma, with the remark—I am indulging in no hackneyed joke, but narrating a simple fact—that she strongly objected to a volume containing such abomination as the foregoing, and preferred that her daughter should restrict her poetical reading to Mr. Tupper. The man who wrote "Vivien," and the parting scene between Guinivere and Lancelot, has not invariably been a moral milkman. Mr. Tennyson

has such immense skill as a craftsman, that he
successfully passes off upon proper people what
they would call shocking improprieties if pro-
ceeding from a less dexterous hand. Therefore,
if all that Mr. Swinburne is pleading for in his
defence of something " that cannot be lisped in
the nursery or fingered in the school-room," be
only the free delineation of sexual passion, I am
bound to say that Mr. Tennyson, in his more extreme moods, and the Hon. Robert Lytton, in his
ordinary ones, have both anticipated him, and
thus blunted the force of his literary complaints.
It is true that neither of them has indulged in
quite such warm language as Mr. Swinburne;
but that is an affair of relative colouring, not a
matter of substance, subject, or principle. As
far as Mr. Lytton is concerned, one has only to
glance at " The Wanderer," *passim*, for a proof
of the assertion; and surely such lines as—

> " O love ! O fire ! once he drew
> With one long kiss my whole soul thro'
> My lips, as sunlight drinketh dew,"

from the " Fatima," from which we have already
quoted, or,

> " And then they were agreed upon a night
> (When the good king should not be there) to meet

> And part for ever.   Passion-pale they met
> And greeted : hands in hands, and eye to eye,
> *Low on the border of her couch they sat*
> *Stammering and staring,"*

from the "Idylls of the King," are sufficient to exonerate Mr. Tennyson from the imputation of writing only for children and girls, and to prove that he can compete—and in my opinion beat—Mr. Swinburne on his own special ground.

But we must grapple still more closely with the relations existing between the muse of Mr. Tennyson and the muse of Mr. Swinburne, inasmuch as in giving a serious account of the " Poetry of the Period," almost everything turns upon it.   I regard each muse alike as essentially feminine, and will proceed at once to illustrate what I mean.

Let us for a moment step aside from the province of poetry proper, and direct our attention to one in which imagination, however, plays a leading part—the province of prose romance. Is there, or is there not, a palpable difference in the tone, and—if I may be permitted the phrase—the atmosphere, of the novels which for twenty years Sir Walter Scott poured forth with such unexampled vigour for the delectation of the

public, and the novels with which, since the hand
of the great wizard waxed cold, we have been so
copiously favoured? Who can deny that the
difference is not only palpable, but strikingly
palpable? And wherein lies the difference?
There is but one answer to the question. Scott
was manly and masculine; his successors are just
as distinctively feminine. During the last twenty
or thirty years, and more decidedly during the
last ten than the last twenty, and during
the last twenty than during the last thirty,
the heroines of novels have been more important than the heroes; and when they were
not actually intended to be such by their author
or authoress, they have been determinedly
invested with more interest by the general public.
Let us take one single instance, fairly typical of
the tones and tendencies to which I am alluding. Let us compare Sir Walter Scott and Mr.
Anthony Trollope. There we have the whole
matter in a nutshell—the representative novelists
of their time brought face to face and contrasted.
It were sheer waste of time to demonstrate the
self-evident; that, though Scott can of course be
relished by women, girls, and children too, he is
pre-eminently a masculine novelist, writing for

men in a manly spirit, and from a man's point of
view; whilst Mr. Trollope, though he can be
relished by men, scarcely by boys, and much less
by children, is a feminine novelist, writing for
women in a womanly spirit and from a woman's
point of view. It would be easy to point out
how, during the same period, painting and the
stage—matters so distinct from each other as
never necessarily influencing one the other—have
experienced, as I have already hinted, a like
change. On the stage, adventure, heroic courage,
variety of passion—Shakespeareanism, in a word
—have had to give way to plays in which
domestic sentiment and all that is expressed by
the phrase "the female element" have predominated. The walls of the Royal Academy,
too, have annually told a similar tale. Mothers,
wives, daughters, babies, dolls, in every conceivable touching condition; soft, sentimental
canvasses, made still more alluring by pathetic,
not to say mawkish, titles, have year after year
asserted their supremacy over the grand, the
heroic, and the manly. When did Scott die?
Almost to a year when Mr. Tennyson began to
write. And had there, meanwhile, whilst Scott
was writing his novels, been no manly poets?

Scott himself is the manliest of bards, though he writes of women with all that delicate grace of which the truly manly pen alone is capable. And what of Byron? We well may say, "he was a man." Some people think he was more, and regard him as a devil. A critic by no means extravagantly favourable to him talks of his "demoniac sublimity." At any rate, he was no moral milkman, and never shirked dealing with sexual passion or sentiment. But he was not for ever harping upon it.

> "For Love is in man's life a thing apart;
> 'Tis woman's whole existence,"

he sings; and he proved the truth of the first line, as far as he was himself concerned, by his "Cain," his "Manfred," his "Childe Harold," and most of his dramas. And Wordsworth? "The worthiest objects," Wordsworth writes, " of the exertion of the faculty of imagination are man's natural affections, his acquired passions"—an untenable distinction, of course, between natural and acquired; but let that pass —"his moral and religious sentiments, and the external universe." But why pursue the subject? Even if any should challenge the assertion that there were giants in those days, they surely will not deny that at least there were men. In these, as far as the faculty of the imagination and the objects on which it is exerted are concerned, we have, as novelists and poets, only women or men with womanly deficiencies, steeped in the feminine temper of the times, subdued to what they work in, and ringing such changes as can be rung on what—I mean no disrespect or depreciation of the sex, that is both fair, devout, dear, and indispensable—has well been called "everlasting woman." Open Mr. Tennyson's first volume, and read the table of contents straight off: " Claribel," " Lilian," " Isabel," " Mariana," " Madeline," " Adelmine," and so on. What are " The Lady of Shalott," " Oriana," " Fatima," " Eleanore," " Œnone," " The May Queen," " The Miller's Daughter," " The Gardener's Daughter," " Lady Clara Vere de Vere," " Love and Duty," " Locksley Hall," and the rest, all about ? All about woman. What is " Maud " about ? Woman. What is "The Princess" about ? Woman, woman. What are the four " Idylls of the King " about ? Woman, woman, woman, woman.   I wonder what the Flos Regum Arthurus and all the Table Round would have thought had they known that their names and deeds would have served this one small purpose in the nineteenth century. I think they would have somewhat grimly smiled as they clanked their spurs and rattled their spears.

But what has Mr. Swinburne got to do with all this ? Surely a great deal. He has tried hard, I grant, and very meritoriously, to shake off "love's fits and fevers," and to sing something more " worthy of men, large, liberal, sincere." He must have an inkling, at least, of what I am urging, since he thus makes Althæa address Meleager :

<blockquote>
"For with time
Blind love burns out ; but if one feed it full,
Till some discolouring stain dyes all his life,
He shall keep nothing praiseworthy, nor die
The sweet wise death of old men honourable,
Who have lived out all the length of all their years
Blameless, and seen well-pleased the face of God,
And without shame and without fear have wrought
Things memorable ; and while their days held out,
In sight of all men and the sun's great light
Have gat them glory."
</blockquote>

Accordingly, in " Atalanta in Calydon," from which the above is taken, and in some shorter poems, Mr. Swinburne has striven to get away from " Laus Veneris" and " Our Lady of Pain,"

and give the world assurance of a man. But
with the exception of the lyrical portions—of
which more anon—I cannot think, despite the
copiousness of his language and the intensely
classical air of these compositions, that he has
here been really successful as an original poet.
They are too obviously, literally, and slavishly
Greek, to reap the meed due to spontaneous
song. Anybody fairly, but not exhaustively,
acquainted with such Greek dramas as have come
down to us, would, in reading the foregoing
passage, of a certainty conclude, if he were told
nothing about it, that it was a translation from
some Greek play. Turn to whatever page we
will in "Atalanta in Calydon," the same thing
strikes us, even though we know we are reading not even a paraphrase but a presumedly
original poem :—

> " Child, if a man serve law through all his life,
>   And with his whole heart worship, him all gods
>   Praise ; but who loves it only with his lips,
>   And not in heart and deed desiring it,
>   Hides a perverse will with obsequious words,
>   Him Heaven infatuates, and his twin-born fate
>   Tracks, and gains on him, scenting sins far off,
>   And the swift hounds of violent death devour."

Here it is Althæa that speaks ; but the utterance of Meleager is pitched in precisely the same key :—

> " O mother, I am not fain to strive in speech,
>   Nor set my mouth against thee, who art wise
>   Even as they say, and full of sacred words.
>   But one thing I know surely, and cleave to this :
>   That though I be not subtle of wit as thou,
>   Nor womanlike to weave sweet words, and melt
>   Mutable minds of wise men as with fire,
>   I too, doing justly and reverencing the gods,
>   Shall not want wit to see what things be right.
>   For whom they love and whom reject, being gods,
>   There is no man but seeth, and in good time
>   Submits himself, refraining all his heart."

Could anything more resemble the substance and language of a Greek drama than these cold, statuesque, stately passages ? But that is their very vice, if we are to consider Mr. Swinburne's claims as an original poet. All this is sheer and mere imitation—imitation of the very best kind, no doubt, but still nothing more; and in producing it Mr. Swinburne is only the slave of his school days, and that selfsame spirit of the age which, vexed and mortified at having nothing grand and heroic of its own to say, turns its poetic eyes to the past, and has compelled so many of its men of letters to " do" translations of the great bards of Hellas. Mr. Tennyson, in

his "Œnone," has done something more than
this, infusing a modern flavour into an ancient
and classic theme, and, in my opinion, has by
that one short fragment surpassed all that Mr.
Swinburne has written of the avowedly classical
kind. (For, as we shall see later, Mr. Swinburne's
own real genius is of anything but a classic, and,
least of all of a Greek turn.) For the present,
however, I wished only to note what it is he has
done outside the sexual region in which his
genius most loves to disport, and in which it has
had its most conspicuous successes; and we arrive
at the conclusion that he has not done much
there worth speaking of as original poetry. For
the real truth is, his muse is like that of
Anacreon: he wants it to sing of the sons of
Atreus, and to discourse of Cadmus, but it will
discourse only of Love. There at once is its
weakness. It is a feminine muse.

But surely, it will be said, Mr. Swinburne's
muse is not a feminine muse in the same sense
that Mr. Tennyson's is; and surely he does not
sing of love, woman, and all that is concerned
with and gathers about woman, in the same way
Mr. Tennyson does? Certainly not. But there
is such a thing as the "one step farther," and

Mr. Swinburne has taken it. Again, we must have recourse to our writers of prose romance, to those who exert the faculty of imagination in novels. I have spoken of Mr. Anthony Trollope, and have called him a feminine novelist,* at the same time pointing him out as the fair analogue, in prose novels, of Mr. Tennyson. Now, Mr. Trollope is a very "proper" writer, as no doubt in manner and usually in matter Mr. Tennyson also is. But is Mr. Trollope the only feminine novelist of the time? And are all the feminine novelists of the time as "proper" as himself? More than that: are not the most "improper" of them—we are obliged to use the word in vogue, in order to be understood, though we wish to convey no ethical opinion of our own in doing so —are not the most "improper" of them not only feminine, but actually women? Mr. Trollope writes of love, still love; but it is the sentimental love of youths and maidens, of coy widows and clumsy, middle-aged men, beginning in flirtation and ending in marriage. In a word, it is pretty,

* I am well aware that Mr. Trollope would himself stoutly deny the correctness of this view; and anybody acquainted with him would doubtless pronounce him to be manliness personified. But the world is stronger than any one man; and it has compelled him to write according to its humour.

pious, half-comical, domestic love—love within the bounds of social law. But what is the love of which many of our men-novelists—men, at least, as far as nominal sex is concerned, though certainly not men as authors or in any literary sense—and nearly all our women-novelists, so freely discourse? It is the love—had we not better call it the lust—which begins with seduction and ends in desertion, or whose agreeable variations are bigamy, adultery, and, in fact, illicit passion of every conceivable sort under every conceivable set of circumstances. Nor have I yet given to the matter its full proportions. In the novels to which I refer, and they may be counted by hundreds, it is not men so much as women who are represented as the leading tempters. The heroines are more animal and impassioned than the heroes. We take up the last number of a well-known weekly review, and we turn to its notices of recent novels. "Trials of an Heiress." By the Hon. Mrs. G. R. Gifford. I have not read this particular novel myself, but what do we find the critic saying of it? "If there is any marked characteristic in the book, it is the strong tendency of the women to make love to the men." In one respect, at least, the

criticism is carelessly beside the mark. The
strong tendency of the women to make love to
the men cannot possibly be the marked characteristic nowadays of any individual novel, since it
is the marked characteristic of most of them.
Within the last few years three or four novels, if
not more, all by ladies, have been withdrawn from
circulation almost as soon as they were published,
on account of this "feminine" propensity having
been thought by the circulating libraries to be in
their case a trifle too warmly done. But the
result was that what few copies could be got hold
of were in immense demand; and the very fact
of their being written proves the condition of our
imaginative atmosphere. What is it that we are
seeing simultaneously in a sister art ? The nude
—we ought rather to say the undressed, for there
is a vast difference between the two—rapidly
threatening to displace the purely domestic in
the painting of the period; and whoever has not
lately noticed the disposition in the illustrations
of our serial literature to slide from the sentimental into the sensuous, must either be of foul of
eyes or strangely unobservant. I have fairly
spoken of the expulsion of the heroic or Shakes-
pearean from the stage in favour of dramas of

domestic pathos ; and I have now to add the in-
controvertible fact that domestic pathos is being
ousted by plays expressly composed with the purpose of bringing as many women on the stage as
possible, and of arraying them when there in as
scant garments and displaying as much of their
physical proportions as is consistent with con-
tinued suggestiveness and sustained interest. At
the same moment *La Grande Duchesse de Gerolstein*
is the great theatrical attraction of the day, since
Madlle. Schneider has contrived to unite in her-
self both of the two phenomena of which we have
spoken—a liberal parade of female limbs and the
"tendency of women to make love to men"
carried to its crowning point.   Surely in this
scientific age no one will doubt that all these
things are related, and that the Schneiderism of
the studio, the stage, and the circulating library
are all traceable to the same cause. It is the
feminine element at work when it has ceased to
be domestic; when it has quitted the modest,
precincts of home, and courted the garish light
.at do tense and warm publicity. It is the
fre is any u ment, no longer in the nursery, the
drawing-room, or the conjugal chamber, but
unrestrainedly rioting in any and every arena of

life in which an indiscriminating imagination
chooses to place it. It is the "one step farther"
of which I have already spoken, but a step that
was inevitable and sure to be taken, when the
first wrong step—that of making women too conspicuous in life and literature—had once been
fatally indulged in. Our "proper" feminine
novelists have but led the way for our "improper" feminine novelists; and the, on the
whole, "proper" feminine muse of Mr. Tennyson
was only the precursor of the "improper" feminine muse of Mr. Swinburne. There is nothing
masculine about the one any more than about the
other; or what advantage there is on either side
in that particular lies, as I have said, with the
muse of the former. Both, however, are substantially feminine muses; only one is the feminine
muse of the Hearth, whilst the other is the feminine muse of the Hetairæ.

As such, then—for in assigning Mr. Swinburne his precise position I have only been pur-
suing an indispensable inquiry, and by no means
intending to object to his filling it if he fou of
vacant, or to read him a moral lecture for doing
so — what are Mr. Swinburne's literary and
poetical merits? I have already expressed my

opinion of the value of his statelier and avowedly classical productions. They are the wonderfully faithful echo of a grand poetical literature that flourished more than two thousand years ago; but they are an echo, and nothing more. They are not the poetry of to-day, though they may be, in a sense, part of the " Poetry of the Period." As we may say, they are " Greece, but living Greece no more;" and poetry that is not alive is not poetry at all. Turn we then to those of Mr. Swinburne's compositions which have a more modern flavour; for in spite of a few—very few —plausible facts that might be adduced in support of such a theory, it was from no dead tongues that Mr. Swinburne caught his two main and essentially modern characteristics, lyrical fluency and erotic ardour. The latter half of the nineteenth century has given him these; and in all that constitutes his original genius he is unmistakably its child:

" Why, two nights hence I dreamed that I could see
In through your bosom under the left flower,
And there was a round hollow, and at heart
A little red snake sitting, without spot,
That bit—like this, and sucked up sweet—like this,
And curled its lithe light body right and left,
And quivered like a woman in act to love.

Then there was some low fluttered talk i' the lips,
Faint sound of fierce soft words caressing them—
Like a fair woman when her love gets way.
Ah! your old kiss—I know the ways of it:
Let the lips cling a little; take them off,
And speak some word, or I go mad with love."
Chastelard.

Here there is nothing classical, any more than there is anything masculine. But it is a capital specimen of one of Mr. Swinburne's two individual manners, and is as thoroughly modern and as completely feminine—of the "one step farther" stage—as anything well could be. It is essentially the product of the same age that has given us M. Michelet's " L'Amour" and " La Femme," and to collate small things with great, the everlasting and wearisome articles about women—the most notable of them by the way, written by a woman—in the *Saturday Review*. It is true that the above is spoken by Chastelard, a man—a man! I scarcely like to own sex with him;—but for all that, it is intrinsically feminine (again, be it always understood, when I am applying this word to Mr. Swinburne's compositions, of the "one step farther" stage). In fact, it is Schneiderism rampant in blank verse.

When I turn from his blank verse to his

lyrical, I feel a little puzzled. In order to prove satisfactorily what I am going to say of it, I should have to quote almost every line of lyrical poetry Mr. Swinburne has ever written. This, obviously, I cannot do, nor indeed shall I quote more than a few fragments. Those, however, who are well acquainted with his works will, I fancy, feel the truth of my observations; and I must ask those who are not to believe that, as far as *manner* is concerned, with which we are now mainly dealing, the following stanzas are typical, and almost exhaustive, of Mr. Swinburne's genius when it is most lyrical, most original—in a word, at its best. They are from "Dolores :"—

> "O lips full of lust and of laughter,
>   Curled snakes that are fed from my breast,
> Bite hard, lest remembrance come after,
>   And press with new lips where you pressed.
> For my heart, too, springs up at the pressure,
>   Mine eyelids, too, moisten and burn;
> Ah! feed me and fill me with pleasure
>   Ere pain come in turn.
>
> "Ah! beautiful, passionate body,
>   That never has ached with a heart!
> On thy mouth, though the kisses are bloody,
>   Though they sting till it shudder and smart,

More kind than the love we adore is,
   They hurt not the heart or the brain,
O bitter and tender Dolores,
    Our Lady of Pain !

" As our kisses relax and redouble,
   From the lips and the foam and the fangs,
Shall no new sin be born for man's trouble,
   No dream of impossible pangs ?
With the sweet of the sins of old ages
   Wilt thou satiate thy soul as of yore ?
Too sweet is the rind, say the sages—
    Too bitter the core."

It is unnecessary to point out that here, again, it is essentially a feminine muse that is sweeping the chords. But what I wish now to note as characteristic of this and all Mr. Swinburne's lyrical poetry is, that it consists of voluble variations on one small theme. There are no less than fifty-five stanzas like the foregoing in this one poem of " Dolores," and these are all so thoroughly alike, save for the shuffle, so to speak, of the words, that any three would have served my purpose just as well as any other three, and the whole fifty-five best of all; for it would then be seen that no distinct impression is left by any one of them as opposed to any other. When we have once read the opening lines :

> " Cold eyelids that hide like a jewel,
>   Hard eyes that grow soft for an hour;
> The heavy white limbs, and the cruel
>   Red mouth, like a venomous flower:
> When these are gone by with their glories,
>   What shall rest of thee, then—what remain,
> O mystic and sombre Dolores,
>   Our Lady of Pain ?"

we already know all about it. The remaining fifty-four stanzas are mere *fioriture;* shakes and quavers, runnings up and down the scales, displaying wonderful facility and flexibility, but giving us no new air, nor even any genuine modification of the air. Indeed, anybody reading " Dolores" through must feel puzzled to know, when he reaches the end, why it is the end; why, in fact, Mr. Swinburne did not go on for ever in that strain. There is no question but that, short of physical exhaustion, he could do so, as he proves that he could when he sets to work to write some fresh lyric, precisely like the one we have quoted from. I may go farther, and safely assert that, with a little practice, Mr. Swinburne might become an improvisatore, and extemporise any quantity of verse like the foregoing. For it is *vox, et præterea nihil*—a voice and nothing more; a most melodious, surprising

voice, no doubt, but so recklessly exercised
and employed that it reminds us of the noise
made by a prepared quill blown in a glass of
water rather than of the song of a bird, much
less of a human throat. Paganini was before
my time, but I believe one of his most popular
performances was to fiddle on one string. I
never heard, however, that he always fiddled on
one string. That was a feat left for Mr. Swinburne to perform, and in a most marvellous
manner does he perform it.

If we turn to a " Song of Italy," precisely
the same effect is produced on the mind of the
reader, and precisely the same criticism provoked.
It is sheer poetical babble; wondrously good
poetical babble, but still only babble. To use a
colloquial phrase, there is nothing in it. Take
away its music and its plash and flutter of words,
and it is utterly unworthy of the subject, and
miserably inadequate. What we call sparkling
wine the Italians call *vino spumante*, and this is
what they would call his " Song" if they read it.
It is *spumante*, sparkling and frothy, but with
no body in it. It abounds in foam, but we look
in vain for the breakers. I may say of it what
Mr. Tennyson says with such abominable extra-

vagance of the Pleiads—that the words glitter
through the strain "like a swarm of fire-flies
tangled in a silver braid." But though fire-flies,
as any one knows who has seen them in perfection
on a southern summer night, are bewitchingly
beautiful, they yield no light to speak of; and
no light to speak of is to be had from Mr. Swinburne's "Song of Italy." Should anybody be
inclined to reply, that froth, glitter, and fire-flies
are best suited to a Song of Italy, let him remember Dante, Tasso, Ariosto, and Alfieri, to
say nothing of the grand, heroic, masculine deeds
recorded in Italian history, and discreetly hold
his peace. Or should that fail to silence him,
let him turn to Byron's "Prophecy of Dante"
and Mrs. Barrett Browning's "Casa Guidi Win-
dows," and there see how Italy can be sung.
Neither will it avail Mr. Swinburne to plead that
the essence and spirit of lyrical poetry reside
rather in its manner than its matter, and that
the accusation of there being "nothing in it" is
irrelevant. Mr. Swinburne himself would be
scarcely likely, on reflection, to employ or accept
any such plea. His classical knowledge would
save him from so foolish an apology. Moreover,
the shade of Shelley, whom he very properly

calls divine whilst improperly arrogating that epithet to him exclusively, would rise in judgment against him. What more perfect specimen of lyrical poetry exists in any language than the "Ode to a Skylark"? Yet there is stuff enough, thought, matter enough in it, to furnish forth more poets, if it only happened to be their own, than have been born into this world since Shelley wrote it.

Mr. Swinburne is very wroth with Mr. Matthew Arnold for making the admirable distinction—all Mr. Arnold's criticisms are admirable, being at once profound and pellucid—that Shelley too often only tries to render what he has got to say, whereas Byron invariably renders it. The remark is obviously true, when once made; and here we find a corroboration of the distinction between the masculine and feminine elements in poetry. For "I know what I mean, but I cannot say it," is essentially a feminine argument and habit; and Shelley, whom probably I admire within the bounds of reason quite as much as Mr. Swinburne does, was infected with this feminine fault. I am ready to fall down and prostrate myself in worship before the genius of Shelley; but, for all .that, it was he who first began to mean what he could not say, and in that respect set a pernicious example since too amply followed. But Mr. Swinburne, instinctively aware that he must, in his lyrical manner at least, shelter himself under the wings of Shelley if anywhere, is angry at being told that Shelley too often only "tried to render" his thoughts, and retorts that Byron was half a Philistine and "a singer who could not sing." He means a singer who did not and would not screech, as poor Shelley now and then unfortunately did; and who positively *could not* indulge in those falsetto notes which appear to compose most of Mr. Swinburne's emasculated poetical voice.

This, then, is the summary of the " Poetry of the Period " as far as Mr. Tennyson, Mr. Browning, and Mr. Swinburne are concerned. No man, despite all the nonsense that has been written to the contrary, and therefore no poet, can, as far as *work done* is concerned, be greater than the age in which he happens to live. It might as well be supposed that a man, by the use of his muscles, could throw a stone farther than the law of gravitation under the circumstances permitted, or by dint of shouting be heard a longer way off than was consistent under the circum-

stances with the law of acoustics. Every individual that comes into the world, no matter how
great his natural gifts, is just as much affected
and limited by the atmosphere of his time as is
a shrub by the climate or season in which it
flourishes. To suppose the contrary is not to
have thought about the matter at all. Mr.
Tennyson, Mr. Browning, and Mr. Swinburne
are mental phenomena of the period—a period
which, however distinguished for smaller characteristics, is incapable of doing really great deeds
or producing really great poetry. The age
plunges into its domestic concerns, its maidens,
its undergraduates, its gardens, its pretty little
streams, its husbands and wives, their quarrels,
reconciliations, and bereavements, its love-making,
and semi-mystical attempts at what it thinks
religion; and forthwith it finds a voice in Mr.
Tennyson. Anon it waxes discontented with
itself and rebellious against the pettiness of its
narrow circle and its pious domestic interests,
puts the latch-key of home into its pocket, sallies
forth with a determination to be a free man again,
and plunges into a course of naughty dissipation.
Mr. Swinburne now is its spokesman. Disgusted
with itself even more perhaps for its brief in-

dulgence in the second mood than for its long submission to the first, it then thinks it would like to betake itself to books, study, deep thought, and analyzing—analysis of itself mostly, for it is a terrible egotist and a very sickly one. Then Mr. Browning comes to the front, and he, too, is equally welcome. Student, domestic character, and sensualist—behold the three *rôles* our age is capable of playing. A really great part is beyond it. Really great song is therefore, and inevitably, equally so. Studious moments are not poetical ones, and Mr. Browning, the representative of the studious moments of the age, is, as we have seen, not specifically a poet at all. Domestic proclivities are quite pretty and pathetic enough to be poetical; and Mr. Tennyson, their representative, is the Poet of the Hearth. Poetical, too, may be the insurrectionary temper which, flinging hotly aside the restrictions so sweetly expressed in the last of the " Idylls of the King," when Arthur addresses Guinivere—

" For I was ever virgin save for thee"—

or represents his knights as swearing

 " To lead sweet lives in purest chastity;
 To love one maiden only, cleave to her"—

resolves to fly to those whom it can address in
the following very different fashion :—

> " Hast thou told all thy secrets the last time,
>   And bared all thy beauties to one?
> Ah! where shall we go then for pastime,
>   If the worst that can be has been done?
> But sweet as the rind was the core is;
>   We are fain of thee still, we are fain,
> O sanguine and subtle Dolores,
>   Our Lady of Pain!"

Poetical, I say, may be this tendency likewise,
and the age has strongly exhibited it. In this
frame of mind, Mr. Swinburne is its poetical
oracle. Higher and grander frames of mind
than the foregoing the period has not, or it
would have higher and grander poetry. Mr.
Tennyson and Mr. Swinburne are such as their
age makes them, or at least permits them to be.
It is not their fault, but only their misfortune—
and ours.

Mr. Matthew Arnold. Mr. Morris.

IT may seem an ungracious, and certainly it is no pleasing, task, to approach the poetical productions of those who have added to our store of mental and spiritual pleasure in other than a spirit of grateful appreciation. To criticise what you have not paid for has never been esteemed an amiable course, and grace rather than cavilling would appear to be tho fitting return for meals gratuitously provided. If gift-horses are not to be looked in the mouth, surely the Pegasus of the Poet, the freest possible gift to all mankind, should not be subjected to too rigorous an inspection. Would it not be better, then, to be blind to the defects and shortcomings of those singers, whom we really feel to be such, and to confine ourselves to an indiscriminating

love of their beauties and an unquestioning admiration of their merits? If comparisons are
odious, of whom could they be more odious than
of poet with poet? When a woman's loveliness
is the theme of praise, is it not the height of
ill-manners to decry her form because some other
woman's is more faultless, or to depreciate her
face because a second can be named whose coun-
tenance is still more radiant? What companion
is there more detestable than he who, when you
are wrought to a pitch of ecstatic delight over
some glorious natural prospect, intrudes on your
enthusiasm with the untimely reminder that it is
not so varied as such an one, or not so extensive
as such another? Why then, instead of joining
in the chorus of praise which surges round the
really precious verse of Mr. Tennyson, or in the
somewhat less loud but equally intense clamour
of welcome which has greeted the muse of Mr.
Swinburne, do I rebuke the ardour of their worshippers, and go out of my way to protest that,
though reasonable commendation is well bestowed
upon each of them, there is such a thing as unreasonable commendation, and that it is being
most recklessly lavished on what they have contributed to the literature of their country? Why

can I not be content to take them for what they
are, and be thankful, mildly abstaining from any
inquiry into what they are not?

The objection is a natural one; but it is very
easily answered. Criticism—or what is so termed
—makes criticism necessary. Did the admirers
of living poets confine themselves to a just and
popular appreciation of their qualities, it is obvious
there would be no room for such protests as we
have thought it our duty to make. I may add
that just as little would there have been any
temptation to make them. It is foolishly extravagant praise, and unweighed words of adula-
tion, that compel one to interfere. It is when a
crowd of unjudicial and injudicious people indulge in such language as has been well embodied
by the first of the two poets whose names are at
the head of this chapter—

> "Tempts not the bright new age,
>   Shines not its stream?
>   Look! ah, what genius,
>   Art, Science, wit!
>   Soldiers like Cæsar,
>   Statesmen like Pitt!
>   Sculptors like Phidias,
>   Raphaels in shoals,
>   Poets like Shakespeare—
>   Beautiful souls!"—

that the critic who has learned to strike something like a fair balance between the efforts of
competing genius, waxes indignant at such preposterous pretensions, and prays some of these
wonderful modern phenomena to come down a
little lower.   Is General Grant a soldier like
Cæsar? Was Baron Marochetti like Phidias, and
are Mr. Leighton, Mr. Millais, or Mr. Anybody
else you may choose to mention with R.A. at the
end of his name, equal to Raphael? Poets like
Shakespeare! Let us not talk of it; the thing
grows too absurd. Yet these are the absurdities
we are constantly compelled to read—not perhaps
always distinctly asserted, but tacitly assumed—
in the critical jargon of the period. I think it
might rouse the very stones to mutiny. I, at
least, have been no longer able to sit quiet
under it.

Moreover, if any apology be required, which
I very much doubt, unless it be by those whose
extravagance has provoked my protest, and whom
my protest naturally irritates, it should be remembered that, over and above the attempt here
made to vindicate the fame of really great poets
dead and gone, my aim has likewise been to
couple the poetry of to-day with the day that

produces it, and, whilst assigning it its due place, to account for the fact of its being no better and greater than it is. Not in any spirit of depreciation, but from a sense of justice mingled with the analyzing mind I suppose I borrow from the age in which I write, have I been urged to this particular investigation.

None the less, however, is the indication of the shortcomings of living poets, whom it would be an unmixed gratification only to praise, a distasteful function; and never could it be more distasteful than in discoursing of the works of two such writers as Mr. Matthew Arnold and Mr. William Morris. Should these pages ever meet their eye, I pray them to believe that I regard their works with extreme reverence. In the case of Mr. Matthew Arnold, one experiences an additional repugnance to the undertaking I have conscientiously imposed on myself, because he himself evidently sees and feels—what is there that he does not see and feel?—the force of all the objections I have to make to contemporaneous verse (his own included), and likewise the uncritical temper in which it is usually mentioned. The sardonic lines I just now quoted show how strongly he disapproves the improper mentioning in the same breath of the giants of old with the pigmies of to-day; and those which he prefixes to the second volume of his "Poems" are of themselves enough to demonstrate in what estimation he holds the poetry, either actual or possible, of such an age as that in which it is his lot to live :—

> "Though the Muse be gone away,
>   Though she move not earth to-day,
>   Souls, erewhile who caught her word,
>   Ah! still harp on what they heard."

He cannot bring himself to refrain from song, but he owns in his inmost heart that there is that without him, if not within him, which will prevent it from being such as was possible before the Muse had gone away. Again and again he recurs to this painful—this overwhelmingly sad conviction. In some of the most exquisite and pathetic lines he ever wrote, " Stanzas from the Grande Chartreuse," it is not only faiths that are dead and gone, but the paralysis which smites the lyre in the interval between their disappearance and some hoped-for palingenesis, that moves him to this mournful strain :—

> " Wandering between two worlds, one dead,
>   The other powerless to be born,

> With nowhere yet to rest my head,
> Like these, on earth I wait forlorn.
> Their faith, my tears, the world deride;
> I come to shed them at their side.
> *   *   *   *   *   *
> There yet, perhaps, may dawn an age,
> More fortunate alas! than we,
> Which without hardness will be sage,
> And gay without frivolity.
> Sons of the world, oh haste those years,
> But till they rise allow our tears!"

He goes about the world, oppressed with the sense not only of the unjoyous, but of the un-spiritual character of the times in which he has been given his brief span of life. Even when Empedocles is the supposed spokesman, it is still Mr. Arnold that speaks through him :—

> " And yet what days were those, Parmenides!
> *   *   *   *   *   *
> Then we could still enjoy, then neither thought
> Nor outward things were closed and dead to us,
> But we received the shock of mighty thoughts
> On simple minds with a pure natural joy.
> *   *   *   *   *   *
> We had not lost our balance then, nor grown
> Thought's slaves, and dead to every natural joy."

Mark the distinction he draws between being Thought's slaves and "receiving the shock of

thought"—a distinction recalling Wordsworth's
"Thought was not; in enjoyment it expired,"
quoted by me when protesting against Mr.
Browning's deep thoughts being considered
poetry—and a distinction which, moreover,
eminently corroborates the position I have
persistently maintained, whilst insisting on the
specific nature of poetical genius. Burning to
bring back such days, and to be no longer
Thought's slave, Mr. Arnold confesses, with sad
reiteration, the vanity of his desires. No amount
of knowledge, no profundity of research, will give
him the poet's strong, free, spontaneously soaring
pinion.   Indeed, they help only to weigh him
down to the ground :—

> "Deeply the poet feels! but he
>   Breathes, when he will, immortal air,
>   Where Orpheus and where Homer are.
>   In the day's life, whose iron round
>   Hems us all in, he is not bound;
>   He escapes thence, but we abide.
>   Not deep the poet sees, but wide!"

Here again we meet with a striking confirmation of the contrast I have pointed out between
deep thoughts and lofty thought—a contrast
which, it is plain, haunts Mr. Arnold, and the

consciousness of which is to him the explanation of his own comparative powerlessness, and of that of his poetical contemporaries. They are all hemmed in and cannot escape. They abide, and cannot mount to breathe the immortal air where Orpheus and where Homer are. The age, not great, but big and exacting, forbids them to geu beyond its influences; and its most imperative influences are those which fasten men down, not those which lend them buoyancy. And what is worst and most grievous of all is that all the poet's efforts to baffle them are bootless :—

> "And long we try in vain to speak and act
> Our bidden self, and what we say and do
> Is eloquent, is well—but 'tis not true!
> And then we will no more be rack'd
> With inward striving, and demand
> Of all the thousand nothings of the hour
> Their stupefying power.
> Ah yes, and they benumb us at their call."

Enormous is the power of the age over us; but it is "stupefying," and Mr. Arnold feels that it has, in a sense, benumbed him far more than it has benumbed all save the chosen few whom he resembles. In order not to be so affected by it, one must remain aloof from it. Yet with what

result ? Let Mr. Arnold himself answer in his
" Stanzas in Memory of Obermann." After a
laconic and somewhat unsatisfactory reference to
Wordsworth as one of the only two spirits besides
Obermann who have seen " their way in this our
troubled day," he goes on to acknowledge—

> " But Wordsworth's eyes avert their ken
>   From half of human fate "—

and to explain that if his spirit was freer from
mists, and much clearer than ours, it was
because

> " . . . though his manhood bore the blast
>   Of a tremendous time,
>   Yet in a tranquil world was passed
>   His tenderer, youthful prime."

To us tranquillity and a tremendous time have
both been denied ; and we cannot avert our ken
from what is now to be seen, even if we would :

> " But we, brought forth and rear'd in hours
>   Of change, alarm, surprise—
>   What shelter to grow ripe is ours ?
>   What leisure to grow wise ?
>
>   Like children bathing on the shore,
>   Buried a wave beneath,
>   The second wave succeeds before
>   We have had time to breathe."

It is ever with him the same complaint. The tree of knowledge of which we have been forced to partake, is no more the tree of song than it is the tree of life. We know all—or we think we do—but all that we can effect with our knowledge is to sigh under the burden of it. The age is sick with a surfeit of analysis, and Mr. Arnold is sick along with it. Not content with half, we have grasped the whole; and, having got it, we have only proved the truth of the old admonition, that the half is often more than the whole. We should like to throw it away, but we cannot; so we keep harping on our disappointment. When Chaucer wrote, and even when Spenser, then could men " still enjoy." Came the times of Shakespeare and Milton, and they could act—not with paralysing infirmity of purpose—not with benumbing doubts, firstly, as to whether they ought to act at all, and, secondly, whether the way in which they were acting was the right way —but with a grand, confident, powerful conviction that there was a particular work to do, and they were the particular men sent to do it. In such an age the poet caught the infectious certainty and direct energy of his time, and, deterred by no scruples of his own and no dread

—indeed, no consciousness—of adverse influences, flung the whole of himself, brain, heart, soul, and passion, into his momentous work. Two hundred years were to pass away before any other such epoch was to arrive. The close of the eighteenth and the opening years of the nineteenth century made a period marked by a fervour to which the world had long been a stranger; but the fervour was new, and all its own. It was the fervour of the iconoclast blent with that of the architect. Never was there an age so bent on destruction; but it destroyed in the burning faith that it could build again, and build better. Politics, constitutions, social ties, humanity itself, were to be reconstructed and reorganized. The old gods were to be dethroned, but new ones, and new ones that should reign for ever, were to take their place.

Some singers caught more the destroying tone, some more the constructive one; but even in the misanthropical splendours of Byron's tremendous strains there is hope, and even with the sanguine mysticism of Shelley's beatific song there blends the anger of divine rage that the old rubbish is not sufficiently quickly carted away, and the rough places made smooth. But none of them hesitated : they were strong and swift, for they were sure ; the native hue of resolution was not sicklied o'er with the pale cast of thought. In Washington Irving's " Tales of the Alhambra," there is a story of a treasure which none could find, though everybody knew it to be there, until at last a happy youth hit upon the exact spot whither the two eyes of a marble statue con- verged ; then the secret was unfolded, and the treasure discovered. So is it with the inward eyes of men : their gaze must converge ; they must look in one and the same direction, or they point to nothing. In what direction is our modern gaze turned ? In two directions, and in each infirmly. One eye glances towards the past, with a feeling partly of love, but still more of dread lest we should have broken with its wisdom ; while the other, with an earnest timidity, strains to find light in the dimness of the future, and ever and anon closes utterly from weariness and despair.

We can no longer believe in Olympus ; and the Pagan theogony and theology, in spite of Mr. Swinburne, are dead for evermore ; whilst as far as that portion of humanity is concerned from which original poetry can ever be hoped for,

Christianity in any sincere sense is virtually just as extinct. To use Mr. Tennyson's words, the most open and sensitive minds now amongst us

> " . . . . sit apart, holding no form of creed,
>   But contemplating all."

We have emptied the heavens and the earth of everything but man and the indefinite unknowable, and stand very properly tolerant in the vacant space we have created. We have made a mental solitude, and call it peace. I mean no reproaches: I am simply stating facts. It is not our fault perhaps, but it is woefully our misfortune. Every thoughtful man and woman feels it; the age feels it; the poet feels it. He, more than any other, is unable to mistake the dead past for the living present; he, more than any other, is unable to mistake what have now proved to be mirages and phantoms for new births and solid promises of the future. "For what availed it," asks Mr. Arnold, in the poem from which we have once before quoted :—

> " For what availed it, all the noise
>   And outcry of the former men ?—
>   Say, have their sons obtained more joys ?
>   Say, is life lighter now than then?"

We have been in the Land of Promise which the fervour of our immediate sires pointed out and fancied they had bequeathed us, and we have found it, some worse, none better, than the desert they bewailed. So, though we inherit the ruins they made, we have no fresh shelter for our heads; past and future alike fail us,

"For both were faiths, and both are gone."

Gone with them, too, says Mr. Arnold, is "the nobleness of grief," and he begs that the "fret" may not be left now that the nobleness is taken away. He is almost ashamed of himself for singing at all. "The best are silent now," he says :—

"Achilles ponders in his tent;
    The kings of modern thought are dumb;
    Silent they are, though not content,
    And wait to see the future come.
    They had the grief man had of yore,
    But they contend and cry no more.
                *   *   *   *   *
"Our fathers watered with their tears
    This sea of time whereon we sail;
    Their voices were in all men's ears
    Who passed within their puissant hail.
    Still the same ocean round us raves,
    But we stand mute and watch the waves."

What wonder, then, that in moments when they cannot be quite mute, nor yet content themselves with bemoaning their impotence, Mr. Arnold, and others like him, should reproduce the literature of the past, and, as he says, now, that " the Muse be gone away," try to " harp on what they heard" ?   In a sonnet to a friend, beginning, " Who prop, thou ask'st, in these bad days, my mind ?" he answers, Homer and Epictetus :—

<blockquote>

               " But be his
My special thanks .   .   .   .

Who saw life steadily, and saw it whole :
The mellow glory of the Attic stage,
Singer of sweet Colonus and its child."
</blockquote>

What must be the mental and spiritual condition of an age, when one of its poets turns away from it to seek his comfort and inspiration in the writings of Sophocles ?   That a student should do so, that a philosopher should do so, that a cynic should do so, were intelligible enough; but a poet !   The Muse must, indeed, have fallen upon evil days, and evil tongues, before this could be ; and that she has done so, is the explanation of the Poetry of the Period.   We have seen how Mr. Swinburne too, when flying from the sensuous atmosphere of

erotic lyricism, can find no refuge but in the
" mellow glory of the Attic stage ;" and the
" something Greek about" Mr. Tennyson's idyllic
manner, has been repeatedly noticed, even to the
extent of some of the recent translators of Homer
having founded their style upon it. We shall see
directly how far the same remark is applicable to
Mr. Morris ; but Mr. Arnold saves us from all
further necessity of investigation, by his " special
thanks," and by the obvious echoes of those
" who prop his mind," in three of his longest
works, " Empedocles on Etna," " Sohrab and
Rustum," and " Balder Dead," and in several
shorter pieces. A very few examples will suffice
to illustrate my meaning :—

> " But as a troop of pedlars from Cabool,
> Cross underneath the Indian Caucasus,
> That vast sky-neighbouring mountain of milk snow ;
> Winding so high, that, as they mount, they pass
> Long flocks of travelling birds dead on the snow,
> Choked by the air, and scarce can they themselves
> Slake their parch'd throats with sugared mulberries—
> In single file they move, and stop their breath,
> For fear they should dislodge the o'erhanging snow—
> So the pale Persians held their breath with fear."
>
> *Sohrab and Rustum.*

> " And as a stork, which idle boys have trapp'd
> And tied him in a yard, at autumn sees

Flocks of his kind pass flying o'er his head
To warmer lands, and coasts that keep the sun—
He strains to join their flight, and from his shed
Follows them with a long complaining cry—
So Hermon gazed and yearned to join his kin."
Balder Dead.

" But an awful pleasure bland
   Spreading o'er the Thunderer's face,
   When the sound climbs near his seat,
   The Olympian council sees !
   As he lets his lax right hand,
   Which the lightnings doth embrace,
   Sink upon his mighty knees.
   And the eagle at the beck
   Of the appeasing, gracious harmony,
   Droops all his sheeny, brown, deep-feather'd neck,
   Nestling nearer to Jove's feet."
Empedocles on Etna.

Why need I point out what these passages sufficiently indicate for themselves ?—that they are the echo of an echo, written less by the Poet than by the Professor of Poetry ; that the writer's mind is leaning upon props, and that here he is not himself ? This may be the verse of the period, but we can scarcely call it the poetry of the period ; it is too academical for that. It is the result and expression of culture, not of impulse. What Mr. Arnold is really like when his impulses master him, we have seen. "Your creeds are dead," he cries :—

> "Your creeds are dead, your rites are dead,
>   Your social order too!
> Where tarries He, the Power who said,
>   *See, I make all things new?*
>
> " . . . . the past is out of date,
>   The future not yet born;
> And who can be alone elate
>   While the world lies forlorn?"

It is in vain and idly that he ascends the "blanched summit bare of Malatrait," there to conclude with an ephemeral effort at being sanguine :—

> "Without a sound,
> Across the glimmering lake,
> High in the Valais depth profound
> I saw the morning break."

Such a conclusion is just as hollow, unsatisfactory, and—I speak objectively—as insincere, as the solution, which is no solution, given by Mr. Tennyson in "The Two Voices," when

> "The sweet church-bells began to peal."

Unhappily, sweet church-bells are no longer any answer to a sad but edifying scepticism that is the martyr of its own candour; and Mr. Arnold proves to us over and over again that he has seen no morning break, and that only those now see it who, like Wordsworth,

> " .   .   .   . avert their ken
> From half of human fate."

In his unrest he gazes at the star-sown vault of heaven, and he gets for answer :—

> "Would'st thou *be* as these are ?   *Live* as they !
> Unaffrighted by the silence round them,
> Undistracted by the sights they see."

But how soon is it before he hears another voice, saying :—

> "Calm 's not life's crown, though calm is well !"

What then is it ?   Mr. Arnold cannot tell us. Neither can the age in which he lives. Homer knew what it was : it was fighting, loving, and singing. Epictetus knew what it was : it was renunciation. Christ knew what it was : it was to leave all things and follow Him. Shakespeare knew what it was : it was, as with the singer of sweet Colonus and its child, to see life steadily, and see it whole. Byron knew what it was : it

was to exhaust and then abuse it.   But we?
But Mr. Arnold?

> "Ah! two desires toss about
> The poets' feverish blood!
> One drives him to the world without,
> And one to solitude."

No doubt they do in these days; but the days
have been when they did not, and when one, and
only one, feverish commanding desire, whatever
it might happen to be, stirred the poets' blood
and ruled it. Otherwise we should have inherited
no greater poetry than now, alas! we can ourselves produce. Great ages, productive of great
things, whatever else may characterise them,
have always this one salient characteristic—that
they have made up their minds. We have not
made up ours, and we cannot make them up.
Two desires toss us about, as they toss about our
poet. The old injunction to steer the middle
course is of no avail here. Mr. Tennyson has
steered it, and we have as a consequence his
golden mediocrity. Mr. Arnold has never been
able to subdue himself to this pitch; and so,
whilst Mr. Tennyson's verse is the resultant of
the many social and spiritual forces of the time,

Mr. Arnold's is fraught with the visible forces themselves, now in its lines expressing one, now another. Anon he makes an effort to submit :—

> " Be not too proud.
> Thy native world stirs at thy feet unknown,
>   Yet there thy secret lies !
> Out of this stuff, these forces, thou art grown,
> And proud self-severance from them were disease.
> O scan thy native world with pious eyes !
> High as thy life be risen, 'tis from these ;
>   And these, too, rise."

But this mood of humble optimism is ephemeral. He chafes at " this stuff," and owns the disease of a yearning for proud self-severance : —

> " The glow . . . . the thrill of life,
>   Where, where do these abound ?—
>   Not in the world, not in the strife
>   Of men shall they be found.

> " He who hath watch'd, not shared, the strife,
>   Knows how the day has gone ;
>   He only lives with the world's life
>   Who has renounced his own."

This last assertion can be accepted only with a most important and pregnant qualification. There is no necessity for a man with high and noble aspirations to renounce his own life in order to live with the world's, if the aspirations of the world at the same time likewise happen to be high and noble. Granted a great age, and a man capable of being great in the direction in which the greatness of the age itself tends, what need of renunciation of one's life then? The age and the man will be one. No two desires will toss either about. They will pull strongly, and pull together. Even this age produces men to whom, not as men, indeed, but under some other connotation, the epithet "great" may be applied. It produces great speculators, great contractors, great millionaires, great manipulators and mountebanks. But poets! Alas! none of these. How can it? It cannot give what it has not got; and it has not got the divine *afflatus*. To live with it, the man who has must indeed renounce his own life; and his own individual possession of the divine *afflatus* helps him not—save to gasp and to flutter. He can do little or nothing, unless the age assists him. He might as well think to fly in vacuum, swim without water, or breathe without air. Mr. Arnold has tried, and feels that he has done that little or nothing—that he has failed; that he had better have remained pondering, like

Achilles in his tent; that the wisest course would
have been to keep silent:—

> " Silent—the best are silent now !"

Turn we now to the singer of, perhaps, the
most unvarying sweetness and sustained tenderness of soul that ever caressed the chords of the
lyre. Whom can I mean, if not Mr. William
Morris, the author of " The Life and Death of
Jason," and " The Earthly Paradise" ?   Even
the critic, accustomed to grasp frail things firmly,
almost shrinks from handling these exquisite
poems with any but the lightest touch, and in
turning them to the light, is fain to finger them
as one does some beautiful fragile vase, the fruit
of all that is at once simple and subtle in human
love and ingenuity. Under a blossoming thorn,
stretched 'neath some umbrageous beech, or
sheltered from the glare of noon by some fern-
crested Devonshire cliff, with lazy summer sea-
waves breaking at one's feet—such were the
fitting hour and mood in which—criticism all
forgot—to drink in the honeyed rhythm of this
melodious storier. Such has been my happy
lot; and I lay before this giver of dainty things
thanks which even the absence of all personal

familiarity cannot restrain from being expressed affectionately. But if we are to persist in our task—if we are really to understand the " Poetry of the Period," we must needs lay aside for awhile the delicacy of mere gratitude, and attempt some more genuine estimate of Mr. Morris's poems than is implied in the fervent acknowledgment of their winsome beaut y. Delightfu as a writer standing by himself and on his own merits, he is invaluable to us when considered along with the other writers whose precise station and significance in poetical literature we have striven to discover : invaluable when we apply to him the test already applied to them, and inquire how comes it that his muse is such as she is, and no other and no greater?

For in Mr. Morris is plain and obvious what in Mr. Tennyson, Mr. Swinburne, and Mr. Arnold has to be made so by some little examination, unravelling, and exegesis on the part of the critic. They halt infirmly and irresolutely between two currents, two influences, two themes. Mr. Morris's poetical allegiance is undivided. Now lured to sing of the Golden Year, now of Œnone —now fancying, as in Aylmer's Field, that a poem of value can be constructed out of the tritest and most threadbare of modern incidents, and now flying back across the centuries in the hope that King Arthur and his Knights may yield more enduring material for the texture of his strains—the Laureate has alternately courted the past and the future, without ever once being able to satisfy our, and, we presume, his own, ineradicable longings for a great contemporaneous poem. In Mr. Swinburne, endowed as he is with more fire and less skill, the results of these conflicting influences are far more apparent, and he is in turns coldly classical and effusively and erotically modern—modern, as of to-day. When we pass to Mr. Arnold, we find him not only likewise a prey to this inevitable distraction —this sundering of the poet's soul in twain, this irreconcilable combat for it between the past and the future, because the present is not strong enough to hold it against the claims of either; but we see him conscious of the raging struggle of which he is the subject and the victim, and conscious whence is derived his impotence, and that of his peers, to wreak full undivided self on song, and produce a great poet linked for all time with a great period. In his own words, he

> "Wanders between two worlds: one dead,
>   The other powerless to be born."

Now, in Mr. Morris we have nothing of this.
He too, like Mr. Arnold, has taken the measure
of the age in which, whatever he will do this
side the "cold straight house," must be done;
but, unlike Mr. Arnold, he has cut himself off
from all its active influences, compounded of
disgust, sanguineness, impatience, and despon-
dency, and has surrendered himself wholly to
the retrospective tendency of his time, which,
when taken by itself, is the most pathetic and
poetical proclivity of which the time is capable.
He ignores the present, and his eyelids close
with a quiet sadness if you bid him explore the
future. He has no power, he says, to sing of
heaven or hell. He cannot make quick-coming
death a little thing; neither for his words shall
we forget our tears. His verses have no power,
he candidly confesses, to bear the heavy trouble
and bewildering care that weigh down the earners
of bread. All he can do is to sing of names
remembered, which, precisely because they are
not living, can ne'er be dead. He finds no life
in anything living, in anything round and about

him; and he feels no impulse to strive vainly to
vitalize them :—

> " Dreamer of dreams, born out of my due time,
>   Why should I strive to set the crooked straight?
>   Let it suffice me that my murmuring rhyme
>   . Beats with light wing against the ivory gate,
>   Telling a tale not too importunate
>   To those who in the sleepy region stay,
>   Lulled by the singer of an empty day."

The realities of the latter. half of the nineteenth century suggest nothing to him save the
averting of his gaze. They are crooked; who
shall set them straight ? For his part, he will
not even try. He knows that effort would be
vain ; and he warns us not

> " To hope again, for aught that I can say."

He feels that he has wings, but all he can do
with them is to beat against the ivory gate. He
sings only for those who, like himself, have given
up the age, its boasted spirit, its vaunted progress, its infinite vulgar nothings, and have taken
refuge in the sleepy region. Not only conscious
of, but vitally imbued with, the truth of Mr.
Arnold's words, when applied to such a period
as this, that

> " He only lives with the world's life
> Who has renounced his own "—

Mr. Morris refuses to renounce the latter, and throws over all the sights, sounds, and struggles of the former, such as they are, to quote Mr. Coventry Patmore, " in those last days, the dregs of Time." Having done so, he invites us to

> " Forget six counties overhung with smoke,
> Forget the snorting steam and piston-stroke,
> Forget the spreading of the hideous town,"

and to forgive him that he cannot case the burden of our fears, but can only strive to build a shadowy isle of bliss in the golden haze of an irrevocable past. Again and again he repeats what it is he can and what it is he cannot do :—

> " Yet as their words are no more known aright
> Through lapse of many ages, and no man
> Can any more across the waters wan
> Behold those singing women of the sea—
> Once more I pray you all to pardon me,
> If, with my feeble voice and harsh I sing,
> From what dim memories may chance to cling
> About men's hearts, of lovely things once sung
> Beside the sea, while yet the world was young."

A certain comparative feebleness there may be in his voice—must be, indeed, in any voice

that is laden with the suppressed sobs of back-
looking regret, as contrasted with one firmly
charged with present messages or confident pre-
sages of a grand approaching future; but harsh-
ness is there none, here or ever, in the strains of
this dulcet client of Apollo.   But whether feeble
or harsh, or whatever to men's ears it may fairly
seem, his muse refuses to wander from the sleepy
region :—

> "Alas! what profit now to tell
> The long unwearied lives of men
> Of past days—threescore years and ten,
> Unbent, unwrinkled, beautiful,
> Regarding not death's flower-crowned skull,
> But with some damsel intertwined
> In such love as leaves hope behind!
> Alas! the vanished days of bliss.
> Will no god send some dream of this,
> That we may know what it has been?"

For all the unprofitable nature of reverting to
these vanished days, he never quits them.   But
he is conscious all the while that it is a strange
thing for a poet, a maker, a seer, to turn his
back on his own time in order to dwell, through
memory, in "that flowery land, fair beyond
words," his love for which, he declares, no scorn
of man can kill :—

> "Thence I brought away
> Some blossoms that before my footsteps lay, .
> Not plucked by me, not over-fresh or bright;
> Yet since they minded me of that delight,
> Within the pages of this book I laid
> Their tender petals, there in peace to fade.
> Dry are they now, and void of all their scent
> And lovely colour; yet what once was meant
> By these dull stains, some men may yet descry,
> As dead upon the quivering leaves they lie."

What beautiful humility in the metaphor! Yet, I am constrained to add, what truth! What delicate loveliness, what rich hues, what lingering fragrance even, in the tales of "The Earthly Paradise," and in the rhymed story of "The Life and Death of Jason"! But, for all that, the delicacy, the colour, the scent, are as of pressed flowers, "not plucked by me." How far short, then, of not being plucked at all, but still bright, dew-sprinkled, odorous, and blossoming

> "In lovely meadows of the ranging land,
> Wherein erewhile I had the luck to stand!"

Mr. Morris knows this, and says it. Still, be they what they may, these dry petals of a bygone world are better than any grown by a present world, that knows only

> "Consuming love,
> Mother of hate, or envy cold,
> Or rage for fame, or thirst for gold,
> Or longing for the ways untried,
> That, ravening and unsatisfied,
> Draws shortened lives of men to hell."

Therefore it is that he chooses his part, and his songs are all of

> "Vain imaginings,
> And memories vague of half-forgotten things,
> Not true or false, but sweet to think upon."

If we turn from the details of "The Earthly Paradise," and regard it in its entirety, we meet with the most remarkable confirmation of the view I am taking, and the view it is impossible not to take—for, just as in Mr. Browning's and Mr. Arnold's cases, it is the author's own—of the scope and limits of his genius. For what is the story, the "argument" of the "Earthly Paradise"? Certain "gentlemen and mariners of Norway, having considered all that they had heard of the Earthly Paradise, set sail to find it," and after many troubles and sore disappointments, come to a "peaceful and delicious land," where they are tended and carried into a city whose denizens are "seed of the

Ionian race," where there are " pillared council-houses" and " images of gold" :—

> " Gods of the nations, who dwelt anciently
> About the borders of the Grecian sea."

I cannot say whether Mr. Morris consciously intended by this outline, and the way in which he fills it up, to typify the yearning shared by him with the age for some immortal poetry or art-production, his own and its utter failure to find them, and their joint discovery in the poetry and art of the nations who dwelt about the borders of the Grecian sea, their greatest and, indeed, their only refuge ; or whether this be a light flung, as has so often before been the case, from the poet's page, without the poet being aware that he had set it there. The point, however, is immaterial, since the similitude, when once pointed out, is too obvious to be missed. I need not repeat what I have said already of the Greek turn of much of Mr. Tennyson's work ; of Mr. Swinburne's entire enslavement, in the non-lyrical portions of his writings, to the Athenian dramatists ; to Mr. Arnold's hankering after the Muse that has gone away ; to the something astir which drives one Prime Minister to translate Homer, and another to publish volumes about the Homeric poems and theology, and which has, moreover, urged so many living men of letters to "do" translations of the bards of Hellas. The facts are too notorious to require more detailed indication.   Like Mr. Morris's "gentlemen and mariners of Norway," now that we see

> "   .   .   .   .   the land so scanty and so bare,
> And all the hard things men contend with there,
> A little and unworthy land it seems,
> And worthier seems the ancient faith of praise."

We have missed what we really wanted ; we have not found for ourselves immortal verse in some hitherto unexplored region; but we are well content, or at least resigned, to find ourselves

> "   .   .   .   .   once more within a quiet land,
> The remnant of that once aspiring band,
> With all hopes fallen away, but such as light
> The sons of men to that unfailing night,
> That death they needs must look on face to face."

Who does not feel how strangely applicable, too, are the following lines to those who have turned from the unfruitful turmoil of the time to the calm study of the serene products of better days ?

> " Yet though the time with no bright deeds was rife,
>   Though no fulfilled desire now made them glad,
>   They were not quite unhappy : rest they had,
>   And with their hope their fear had passed away.
>   *   *   *   *   *   *
>   In such St. Luke's short summer lived these men,
>   Nearing the goal of threescore years and ten !
>   The elders of the town their comrades were,
>   And they to them were waxen now as dear
>   As ancient men to ancient men can be."

So is it with Mr. Morris. So is it with Mr.
Arnold. So is it with the age, or that in it and
us which is alive to poetical impulse and dominion.
The elders have waxen dear to us because we are
ourselves ancient men, in all that concerns the
soul, " with all hopes fallen away." The spiritual
side of us can find nothing akin, nothing to assimilate in " six counties overhung with smoke," in
" the spreading of the hideous town," and all the
mean vulgar passions which material civilisation
calls into supreme play :—

> " Among strange folk they now sat quietly,
>   As though that tale had nought with them to do.
>   *   *   *   *   *   *
>   Yet, since a little life at least was left,
>   They were not yet of every joy bereft,
>   For long ago was past the agony,
>   Midst which they found that they, indeed, must die

> And now well-nigh as much their pain was past,
> As though death's veil already had been cast
> Over their heads—so, midst some little mirth,
> They watched the dark night hide the gloomy earth."

Could there be a more accurate picture of the real " gentlemen and mariners" among ourselves ? They have nursed a beautiful dream ; they have passed through a series of disillusions ; and now among strange folk, among the records and regrets associated with the past, they sit quietly

> " Watching the dark night hide the gloomy earth."

But how can great poetry spring from such a mood or attitude as that ? Impossible—for ever impossible ! Great poetry is the growth of confident creed and fervent or settled passion combined. Great anything cannot be made out of beautiful regrets. What can be made out of them Mr. Morris has made ; and I am sometimes inclined to think that his, after all, is the most valuable, as it is certainly the most definite, contribution to the Poetry of the Period. Mr. Ruskin, in his latest publication, " The Queen of the Air," speaks of Mr. Morris's poems as not quite so beautiful as those of Keats, but displaying a far more powerful grasp of subject. I think the criticism is sound; certainly the latter part of it is. Mr. Morris's grasp is complete—far more so, at least, than that of any other living poet. But that arises entirely from his freedom from that distraction on which I have dilated, and to which all the rest of them are subject. Mr. Morris has given the go-by to his age, and he has done wisely. But in doing so not only has he not produced great poetry—he has evaded the very conditions on which alone the production of great poetry is possible. Even in co-operation with an age—as the present one, for instance—it may be impossible to develope it; but without that co-operation all hope of such is bootless and vain. Exquisitely soothing strains, as of some sweet Æolian harp, may be borne about by the winds that have gently vexed some patient, passive soul; but they have nothing in common with the stirring notes swept by a living hand from the chords of a fresh-strung instrument. These are not for our day. The sweet sadness of things and inevitable death are the constant burden of Mr. Morris's strains, and he chants them with a childlike simplicity that, amid abominable literary affectation and artificialities, has largely helped to deepen the cordiality with which hundreds of the weary have welcomed him. But when I had said all—and it might be much—of his precious contributions to the poetical literature of the time, I should, in justice, still have to estimate how far they were from being great; and less averse from saying it because he himself has said it in all sincerity, I should be compelled to pronounce him, not a great poet, not a mighty maker, not a sublime seer, but at most and at best—

"The idle singer of an empty day;"

the wisely unresisting victim of a rude irreversible current; the serene martyr of a mean and melancholy time.

Roman Catholic Poets.*

NO account of the "Poetry of the Period" would be complete which did not include a prominent notice of its Roman Catholic poets. Not only are they in themselves a singularly significant literary and social phenomenon: they shed a flood of light on one special feature, to which I have not yet referred, in the compositions of those authors whose works we have been considering.

For nothing is more remarkable in the writings of Mr. Tennyson, Mr. Browning, Mr. Swinburne, and Mr. Arnold, than—to use the word in its widest and most catholic sense—the theological

---

* I have felt some little difficulty in fixing the sub-title of this chapter; but the one selected is, I think, the most comprehensive that could have been pitched upon, whilst it certainly is the most accurate.

element which pervades them ; and from those of Mr. Morris it is absent only because, as I have explained, he gives the go-by to the age in which he lives, and sings solely of the times when beliefs were not subjects of contest at all, but matters fixed and unquestioned. The remaining four, however, are perpetually haunted and possessed by the theological problems and disputes which so woefully vex and harass these latter days; and their verse is freighted with ponderous questions as to the origin and destiny of man, the existence and nature of God, the relations of the One to the other, the credibility of Christian doctrine, the respective merits of its various forms, the meaning of death, the likelihood or unlikelihood of immortality, and all the thousand-and-one distressing spiritual inquiries which must beset our souls when once we have ventured, as this age has ventured, on the shoreless sea of ever-undulating doubt.

And be it noticed—for otherwise I should have no occasion to dwell upon it—that this is a new phenomenon in the modern world; meaning by modern, in this instance, the world as transformed and informed by Christianity. In the declining days of paganism, a scepticism, in many respects akin to that we now see around us, embodied itself in verse, as the magnificent poem of Lucretius—which, moreover, does not stand alone—abundantly testifies; but eighteen hundred years were to pass away before the strange spectacle of the Muse having to do duty as a *doctor dubitantium* was to be reproduced. Not that religious subjects, handled even in a somewhat dogmatic spirit, have ever been foreign to the patrons of the lyre. One of the earliest poems by a Christian is the "Evangelicæ Historiæ" of Juvencus, who, in the fourth century, produced a metrical paraphrase of the Gospels, almost timidly scrupulous in its adherence to the sacred text; and nearly two hundred years later, Arator, probably inspired by the success of Juvencus, wrote the "Historiæ Apostolicæ," two books of hexameter verse on the story of the Apostles, which are again little more than a reproduction in metre of portions of the "Acts." Prudentius, too, seeking to atone for a youth and manhood of dissipation by an old age of vigorous orthodoxy, habitually sallied forth, as in his "Apotheosis," his "Hamartigeneia," his "Psychomachia," and his "Contra Symmachum," in the armour of Apollo, to do battle with unbelievers; but though it would be unjust and uncritical to deny him a frequently felicitous style, a lofty diction, and a hearty eloquence, the hazardous assertion of Bentley that he was " the Horace and Virgil of the Christians," is more likely to content the scholar or the devotee than the real lover of poetic inspiration. An impartial judgment will scarcely enrol his rhymed controversies among the genuine bequests of the poetic temper; and if Prudentius must be classed with those who borrow the form in which they write less from the inspiration of their own ideas than from the affectation of the time in which they live, Arator and Juvencus, and their successor in the ninth century, Theodulph, the Italian Bishop of Orleans, have still less claim to be considered as touched with hallowed· fire. Nor can the hymns of the Christian Church—whether we regard those of the Greek Synesius, of the Latin Ambrose, or the English Keble—be adduced with any force to show that an alliance between poetry and special theological forms of belief is common. None of the elegant productions to which I allude would be allotted real poetic rank save by those to whose peculiar religious feelings they happen to give pleasurable vent. The great masters of song, no matter what particulars of their individual creed, have never been habitually hampered by them. Their beliefs were absorbed and well assimilated, and formed the unconscious, unclogging vital force of their mental action, just as the healthy blood lends vitality, and not obstruction, to the exercise of the body's physical functions. The world possesses two great Christian epics—the "Divine Comedy" and the "Paradise Lost;" but though both Dante and Milton are definite enough in all conscience in their theological ideas, these are merely part and parcel of the machinery and very substance of their works; and wherever the second of them, somewhat in obedience to one of the tendencies of his epoch, introduces them gratuitously, everybody has felt that they would be far better away, and only deform a truly sub-lime work. As for Shakespeare, the fact that people still dispute as to whether he was a Roman Catholic or a Protestant is enough to prove that, *quâ* poet, he was neither, "but of all time." Living amid the very clash of furious religious polemics, he instinctively felt that theological opinions are very transitory matters, and that human nature is both above and beyond all

creeds. I need scarcely pursue the subject
farther; and when I have added, in order to
obviate criticism, that Pope's " Essay on Man"
is, as Pope himself strongly insisted, an ethical
and not a theological poem, it may fearlessly be
laid down that, since the days of dying paganism,
there has not till to-day been seen the spectacle
of the poetical literature of an age perpetually
haunted, as I have said, and possessed by a
spirit on which we can bestow no other epithet
than that of theological.

I should be glad to illustrate this particular
point more fully; but it will be so obvious, when
once indicated, to those who are acquainted with
the works in question, that perhaps very brief
references will answer the purpose. When treating of Mr. Tennyson's works, I made but a passing allusion to " In Memoriam," for it is in this
place that it properly demands our notice.
Apart from its other character as a touching
tribute to the memory of a cherished friend, it
may be regarded as a theological poem from
cover to cover. In xxxiv. of the work commences
a long series of questionings and agonizing doubts
about the future state: Is there any future life at
all? If there be, will the consciousness of that

life be continuous with the consciousness of this ?
In replying to the question, an attack is made
upon philosophic pantheism, and certain Christian
forms of mysticism, all of which are declared to
be faiths " as vague as all unsweet." Next the
mystery of evil comes in for treatment, and " Are
God and Nature, then, at strife ?" is asked,
since

> " Nature, red in tooth and claw
> With ravine, shrieks against the creed"

that " God is love indeed." It must remain a
matter of opinion whether Mr. Tennyson has
satisfactorily answered the doubts he states—
whether, to use his own words, he has

> " faced the spectres of the mind
> And laid them."

I am strongly inclined to think that, as Pitt said
of Paley, he has raised more difficulties than he
has solved. The picture of himself as

> " An infant crying in the night,
> An infant crying for the light,
> And with no language but a cry"—

as " faltering where he firmly trod," and as one
who is able only to

> " . . . . stretch lame hands of faith, and grope
> And gather dust and chaff, and call
> To what I feel is Lord of all,
> And faintly trust the larger hope"—

will probably commend itself to those who have learnt to doubt at all, more than will any less hesitating expression of opinion about the after-life to be found in the same poem. And if we conclude that their condition of mind is best represented, when they have closed the volume, by the stanza—

> "O life as futile then as frail !
> O for thy voice to soothe and bless !
> What hope of answer of redress ?
> Behind the veil, behind the veil"—

we probably shall not be far wrong. Mr. Tennyson's only other poem, deliberately and expressly dedicated to the solution of a theological question, is "The Two Voices ;" and its utter ineptitude, regarded from that point of view, has been already explained in the remarks on Mr. Arnold. But scattered through Mr. Tennyson's works will be found continual references to what he calls in one place "The painful riddle of the earth," and in another, the "Something in the world amiss," which "will be unriddled by and by." For, in spite of his own "faint trust in the larger hope"—which would often seem to be faint indeed — he elsewhere shows a decided tendency, borrowed from his time (of which, as I have more than once said, he is the most complete poetical exponent), to look to the future of the race in this world rather than to the future of the individual in another, for the realization of our hopes of human perfectibility. But this matter, too, he leaves unsettled.

> " 'Twere all as one to fix our hopes on Heaven
> As on this vision of the golden year;
> 'Tis like the second world to us that live"—

he writes; and then with a touch of positivism he adds :—

> " . . . . but well I know
> That unto him who works, and feels he works,
> This same grand year is ever at our doors."

Most appropriately, whether with intention or not, the poem finishes thus :—

> " . . . . . . High above I heard them blast
> The steep slate-quarry, and the great echo flap
> And buffet round the hills from bluff to bluff."

For that is just about all we seem to hear when Mr. Tennyson drags into his verse theological and spiritual inquiries as to God and man. His own mind, like that of the period, is in a state of absolute flux; and he leaves those readers whom he influences at all in these matters in a condition precisely similar to his own.

It is chiefly in "Christmas Eve and Easter Day" that the reader will see how far Mr. Browning, whilst aspiring to be a singer, is driven in these days to tackle theological difficulties, and how much light he casts upon them. He can endure, he says, and almost comprehend everything, save what he calls

> "The exhausted air-bell of the critic.
>   Truth's atmosphere may grow mephitic,
>   When Papist struggles with Dissenter,
>   Impregnating its pristine charity—
>   One by his daily fare's vulgarity,
>   Its gust of broken meat and garlic—
>   One by his soul's too-much presuming,
>   To turn the frankincense's fuming,
>   And vapours of the candle, star-like,
>   Into the cloud her wings she buoys on."

But each of these, though perhaps they poison the pure air for healthy breathing, at any rate set it seething :—

> "But the critic leaves no air to poison ;
>   Pumps out by a ruthless ingenuity
>   Atom by atom, and leaves you vacuity."

The reader will probably think the above

quotation only another proof of Mr. Browning's inability to write either poetically or lucidly when striving to be original; but underneath its turbid surface there lies the opinion that Popery and Dissent are just tolerable, but free-thought intolerable altogether. By and by, however, he speaks of his heart as being foolish for expanding

> "In the lazy glow of benevolence,
>   O'er the various modes of man's belief,"

and appears to feel that,

> "Needs must there be one way, our chief
>   Best way of worship . . . . . ."

To find it out, and share it, as far as is possible, with other people, constitutes, he says, his earthly care. He adds however, significantly, that

> "God's is above it, and distinct."

But

> "Lest myself, at unawares, be found,
>   While attacking the choice of my neighbours round,
>   With none of my own made—I choose here!
>   The giving out of the hymn reclaims me."

Here is a pretty muddle of reason and unreason, in all conscience. What it really amounts to is this : that candid scepticism is so disagreeable that he will have'none of it; that Popery and all other forms of belief are untrue, but have some good in them; and that one particular form, equally untrue with the rest, but to whose worship and hymns he is most accustomed, a man had better choose and stick to, rather than be without any at all! In fact, utter theological perplexity, escape from which is to be had by a blind plunge of the hand into a lottery, is the offer of this supposed seer to the afflicted spirits of the period.

What has been already said of Mr. Arnold, Mr. Morris, and Mr. Swinburne, happily precludes the necessity of any prolonged reference in this place to their theological views as manifested in their writings. Mr. Arnold's confession lies in lines already quoted and much dwelt upon.

. "Your creeds are dead, your rites are dead,"

is his piteous exclamation; and his estimate of our spiritual condition and his own is summed up in this sad stanza :—

> " Wandering between two worlds, one dead
>   The other powerless to be born,
> With nowhere yet to rest my head,
>   Like these, on earth I wake forlorn.
> Their faith, my tears, the world deride;
> I come to shed them at your side."

In Mr. Morris's lines—

> " So let me sing of names rememberëd,
>   Because they, living not, can ne'er be dead "—

we are admitted, it would seem, into the very
heart of his mind, and allowed to see that, unwilling to remain in the forlorn state described
by Mr. Arnold, but equally with him convinced
that there is nowhere for him to rest his head in
all that he sees and hears around him, he flies
back to the gods and goddesses of Greece, and
under their imaginary wings craves the shelter
and the peace he can find in no modern divinities.
This Mr. Morris does in all quietness and gentle-
ness of spirit; but over Mr. Swinburne's muse
there comes perpetually a rush of stormy anger
that those gods and goddesses have been dethroned, and a passion of prophecy that the
dethronement is to be followed by restoration :—

> " Will ye bridle the deep sea with reins, will ye
>   chasten the high sea with rods?
>   Will ye take her to chain her with chains, who is
>   older than all ye gods?
>   All ye as a wind shall go by, as a fire shall ye pass
>   and be past;
>   Ye are gods, and behold, ye shall die, and the waves
>   be upon you at last.

> Though before thee the throned Cytherean be fallen,
>   and hidden her head,
> Yet thy kingdom shall pass, Galilean; thy dead shall
>   go down to the dead."

So it is. One poet of the period sighs for the return of paganism, and all "delicate days and pleasant." Another refuses to sing of anything else. A third sings continually of them, and then always with calmness, whilst, when he turns to the faiths of the day, he declares, with a wail of woe, that they are tottering—nay, that they are dead. A fourth bids us stick to the one we happen to be born in, provided it be not "the exhausted air-bell of the critic." And a fifth, the most influential of all, speaks complacently of

> " Sitting, like God, holding no form of creed,
>   But contemplating all;"

and assures us that

> " There lives more faith in honest doubt,
>   Believe me, than in half the creeds."

If than in half, one naturally asks, why not than in all? Or if only than in half, which half? Certainly we have a multiplicity of counsellors;

but in which is there wisdom? Would they not
have shown more sense had they let this particular matter alone altogether—as Shakespeare
did, for instance? But they are poets of the
period, and could not help themselves; and the
above is the outcome of their meddling with it.
Verily, I doubt if either poetry or theology be
any better for their interference:

* * * * *

* * * * *

Now let us turn to some quite different
poetry of the period, but which is as truly its off-
spring and product as anything written by Mr
Tennyson, Mr. Arnold, or Mr. Swinburne. A
monk is dying :—

> " Jesu, Maria—I am near to death,
> And thou art calling me; I know it now."

His friends around him are plunged in prayer to
apostles, evangelists, martyrs, and confessors, to
aid him in his closing hour; and as their impe-
trations cease, he himself takes up the sacred
strain, and spends his final moments in a profession of faith :—

" Firmly I believe, and truly,
    God is Three, and God is One;
And I next acknowledge duly
    Manhood taken by the Son.
And I trust and hope most fully
    In that Manhood crucified;
And each thought and deed unruly
    Do to death, as He has died.
Simply to His grace and wholly
    Light and life and strength belong;
And I love supremely, solely,
    Him the holy, Him the strong.
Sanctus fortis, sanctus Deus,
    De profundis oro te,
Miserere, Judex meus,
    Parce mihi, Domine.

" And I hold in veneration,
    For the love of Him alone,
Holy Church as His creation,
    And her teachings as His own.
And I take with joy whatever
    Now besets me, pain or fear,
And with a strong will I sever
    All the ties which bind me here.
Adoration aye be given
    With and through the angelic host,
To the God of earth and heaven,
    Father, Son, and Holy Ghost.
Sanctus fortis, sanctus Deus,
    De profundis oro te,
Miserere, Judex meus,
    Mortis in discrimine."

With such words upon his lips he dies, but to awake immediately to another life :—

> "I went to sleep; and now I am refreshed.
> A strange refreshment; for I feel in me
> An inexpressive lightness, and a sense
> Of freedom, as I were at length myself,
> And ne'er had been before."

Presently he hears "a heart-subduing melody." It is the voice of his angel-guardian, who thus sings :—

> " My work is done,
> My task is o'er,
> And so I come,
> Taking it home,
> For the crown is won,
> Alleluia,
> For evermore.

> '' This child of clay
> To me was given,
> To rear and train
> By sorrow and pain
> In the narrow way.
> Alleluia,
> From earth to heaven."

When, at last, the angel has ceased his beatific strains, the disembodied soul addresses him, and is by him instructed in the difference between the particular and the general judgment, just as

it is laid down in the theology of the Roman
Catholic Church. Whilst they are discoursing,
there reaches their ears "a sour and uncouth
dissonance." It proceeds from demons :—

> "Hungry and wild, to claim their property
> And gather souls for hell."

Thus the doctrine of eternal punishment, so
shocking to modern Christian ears polite, is distinctly alluded to ; and, indeed, one of the songs
of the guardian angel concludes with " All praise
to Him "

> " Who raises Mary to be Queen of Heaven,
> While Lucifer is left, condemned, and unforgiven."

Into the mouth of the demons is put mocking
language, such as is not unfrequently heard in
terrestrial discourse, and which may not unfairly
be taken as the actual lesson intended to be
inculcated even by Mr. Tennyson's "St. Simeon
Stylites :"—

> " What's a saint ?
> One whose breath
> Doth the air taint
> Before his death :
> A bundle of bones
> Which fools adore,
> Ha ! ha !

When life is o'er,
Which rattle and stink
E'en in the flesh.
From shrewd good sense,
He'll slave for hire,
And does but aspire
To the heaven above
With sordid aim,
And not from love,
Ha! ha!"

" How impotent they are!" exclaims the soul, who hears but cannot see them :—

" I see not those false spirits; shall I see
My dearest Master, when I reach His Throne?"

This he hopes to do, seeing that

".　.　.　.　.　.　. in life
When I looked forward to my purgatory,
It ever was my solace to believe
That, ere I plunged amid the avenging flame,
I had one sight of Him to strengthen me."

The angel assures him that he will :—

" Yes, for one moment thou shalt see thy Lord.
*　　*　　*　　*　　*　　*
One moment; but thou knowest not, my child,
What thou dost ask: that sight of the Most Fair
Will gladden thee, but it will pierce thee too."

After passing through various choirs of

angelicals, who are all singing their appropriate hymns, the soul, conducted by its guardian angel gains the stairs, which rise towards the Presence Chamber :—

> "The smallest portions of the edifice,
>   Cornice, or frieze, or balustrade, or stair,
>   The very pavement is made up of life—
>   Of holy, blessed, and immortal beings,
>   Who hymn their Maker's praise continually."

Accordingly, "Angels of the Sacred Stair" are likewise hymning it, and this is the strain their love pours forth :—

" Father, whose goodness none can know, but they
    Who see Thee face to face,
  By man hath come the infinite display
    Of Thine all-loving grace ;
  But fallen man—the creature of a day—
    Skills not that love to trace.
  It needs, to tell the triumph Thou hast wrought,
  An angel's deathless fire, an angel's reach of thought.
  It needs that very angel, who with awe,
    Amid the garden shade,
  The great Creator in His sickness saw,
    Soothed by a creature's aid,
  And agonized, as victim of the Law,
    Which He himself had made ;
  For who can praise Him in His depth and height,
    But he who saw Him reel in that victorious fight ?"

In another moment the soul is before the judgment-seat, and what the angel-guardian foretold arrives. The sight of the dear Master gladdens but pierces, and the soul instantly swoons. When he reawakes to consciousness, this is his only demaud :—

> "Take me away, and in the lowest deep
>   There let me be,
>   And there in hope the long night-watches keep,
>   Told out for me.
>   There, motionless and happy in my pain,
>   Lone, not forlorn,
>   There will I sing my sad, perpetual strain,
>   Until the morn.
>   There will I sing and soothe my stricken breast,
>   Which ne'er can cease
>   To throb, and pine, and languish, till possest
>   Of its Sole Peace.
>   There will I sing my absent Lord and Love ;—
>   Take me away,
>   That sooner I may rise, and go above
>   And see Him in the truth of everlasting day."

The guardian angel then carries the soul to "the golden prison," where the spirits in purgatory are singing hymns of praise and love to God ; and as he bears him along, he chants the following words, with which the poem concludes :—

" Softly and gently, dearly-ransomed soul,
    In my most loving arms I now enfold thee,
And o'er the penal waters as they roll,
    I poise thee, and I lower thee, and hold thee.

" And carefully I dip thee in the lake,
    And thou, without a sob or a resistance,
Dost through the flood thy rapid passage take,
    Sinking deep, deeper, into the dim distance.

" Angels, to whom the willing task is given,
    Shall tend, and nurse, and lull thee as thou liest;
And masses on the earth, and prayers in heaven,
    Shall aid thee at the Throne of the Most Highest.

" Farewell, but not for ever! brother dear,
    Be brave and patient on thy bed of sorrow;
Swiftly shall pass thy night of trial here,
    And I will come and wake thee on the morrow."

It has been impossible to refrain from copious ·
quotations, since my purpose was to show two
things : firstly, that we have here a very beautiful
and very complete poem ; secondly, that not only
in spirit and tone, but in every detail and particular, we have the most salient, and to Pro-
testants the most scandalizing, doctrines of the
Roman Catholic Church introduced and even
obtruded.   In fact, the whole system of Roman
Catholic theology is here exposed, and employed
as a reality, and a matter so utterly beyond

question as to form the necessary machinery of any dramatic action beyond the grave. And who is the author of this poem? The man in the workings of whose individual mind the intelligent portion of the English public is more interested than in that of any other living person, unless Mr. John Stuart Mill is in this respect to be bracketed equal with him? The name of the poem is " The Dream of Gerontius," and its author is Dr. Newman. Away from the turmoil of life, free from all ambition, possessed by a humility that perhaps has never been rivalled, cut off from the Anglican communion by his abandonment of it, and virtually lost to the Roman Catholic communion by the ignominious jealousy and base dread which its more influential hierarchs in this country entertain of his splendid powers, the author of Gerontius "sits apart," but not " holding no form of creed ;" on the contrary, holding a most definite creed, and *musis amicus* as he is, never taking up even the secular lyre save to infuse something sacred into the strain. He never doubts—he only asserts ; and when he asserts, it is but to reassert, in a manner more personal to himself, the beliefs embodied in the " Dream of Gerontius." To him the month of May is the

month of Mary, and he sings them together.
St. Philip—the head of the order to which Dr.
Newman belongs—is to him a living friend, and
over and over again he addresses him in loving
verse. His own guardian angel, too, is spoken
of as

> " My oldest friend—mine from the hour
>   When first I drew my breath,
>   *   *   *   *   *
> " Mine, when I stand before the Judge;
>   And mine, if spared to stay
> Within the golden furnace, till
>   My sin is burned away.
>
> " And mine, O Brother of my soul,
>   When my release shall come;
> Thy gentle arms shall lift me then,
>   Thy wings shall waft me home."

It is no mere tender woman that writes
thus, but the clearest logician and most skilled
dialectician of his time. In another poem, called
" The Golden Prison," the same sentiments
occur. He is to be saved, he hopes, but saved
by fire. The same turn of mind, though less
distinctly pronounced, is to be seen in poems
written by him before he passed from the fold of
the church in which he was born into that of the

church into which it is now evident he will die.
Traces of it are to be followed up and down the
" Lyra Apostolica," in which the poems signed δ
are all by Dr. Newman. Turn, for instance, to
those under the heading of " Severity," especially
LXXXI., in which he complains bitterly of the soft,
indifferent spiritual temper of the time. As for
contemplating all creeds with a " lazy bene-
volence," he can think of such a state of mind
only to be aroused by it to scorn :—

> " One only way to life:
> One Faith, delivered once for all ;
> One holy Band, endowed with Heaven's high call;
>   One earnest, endless strife !—
> This is the Church th' Eternal framed of old.

> " Smooth open ways, good store ;
> A creed for every clime and age,
> By Mammon's touch new moulded o'er and o'er ;
>   No cross, no war to wage ;
> This is the Church our earth-dimmed eyes behold."

Addressing the religious liberalism of his time,
he tells its disciples—

> " And so ye halve the Truth ; for ye in heart,
>   At best, are doubters whether it be true ;
>   The theme discarding as unmeet for you."

With the spirit of the age he has no sympathy.
It is "a falling age," "a self-flattering age."
England is only the "Tyre of the West." In
one poem he avers—

> "But now I see that men are mad awhile,
>   And joy the age to come will think with me.
>   'Tis the old history: Truth without a home,
>   Despised and slain—then rising from the tomb."

For him there is no "painful riddle of the earth,"
no "something in the world amiss, to be unriddled by and by." Earth is merely a pre-
paration for heaven. The something amiss will
never be righted this side the grave. The
"Golden Year" is an idle dream, and the
"Golden Prison" is the one reality. It never
enters his head to exclaim with Mr. Browning—

> "To be a Christian is hard."

To the forlorn state of Mr. Arnold he is a
stranger; and the dainty divinities of Mr.
Swinburne's imagination figure in his mind only
as a chorus of demons. The poem entitled "The
Greek Fathers" might well have been written
after perusing Mr. Morris's "Earthly Paradise."

> "Let others sing thy heathen praise,
>   Fallen Greece! the thought of holier days
>   In my sad heart abides,"

it begins, and concludes with a glorification of

> "　.　.　.　.　Clement's varied page,
> 　And Dionysius, ruler sage,
> 　　In days of doubt and pain :
> 　And Origen, with eagle eye,
> 　And saintly Basil's purpose high
> 　To smite imperial heresy,
> 　　And cleanse the altar's stain."

In a word, his poetry is not the poetry of doubt and desolation, or even of sweet sadness and the faint trusting of a larger hope. It is the poetry of ardent faith, imbedded in the most astonishingly definite forms that faith has ever assumed.

Nor does he stand alone; otherwise we might perhaps allow ourselves—though in this scientific age there would be some difficulty in the process —to regard Dr. Newman, on his poetic side, as an isolated and unaccountable phenomenon. But he is well attended. Open Mr. Aubrey de Vere's Poems. To whom are they dedicated, to begin with? " To the Very Rev. John Henry Newman, D.D., with the utmost respect and gratitude." They are a fitting tribute, for they breathe the same spirit that pervades "The Dream of Gerontius." Turn to " A Protestant's Musings at Rome." To what conclusion does it please

Mr. Aubrey de Vere to lead the soliloquiser?
That subjection is glorified by the obedience to
God paid through the Pope, his Vicar! That
the Apostles reign at Rome :—

" Reign from their tombs, and conquer from their dust.
Behold the mystery of the ages! . . . .
. . . . History is mad,
Or finds its meaning here. One mystery vast
Solves here philosophy's uncounted riddles :
Time and its tumults here are harmonised :
Hope is here found, or nowhere !
                              As a mist
That strives no longer, swept by quivering winds
From some peaked mountain, my oppression leaves me.
The world is mine once more. Refreshed I rise ;
And gales of life from that celestial bourne
Whereto we tend, strike on me. With soft shock
Yon almond bower lets fall its summer snow."

Look next at the author's sonnets, especially
those " On the Discipline of the Church."
Monastic cloisters, when treated by Mr. Aubrey
de Vere, cut a very different figure from what
they are made to do by Mr. Browning ; as, for
example, in the latter's " Soliloquy in a Spanish
Cloister" :—

" Baths of the Church ! seclusions sad, yet dear ! "

Mr. De Vere calls them, and labels them as

places of sweet refuge for the troubled and the
tired :—

"Alas! world-wearied spirits, fly no more!
  These springs make strong the feeble knees: these
      dews
  Efface the lines of lingering care; infuse
  Immortal youth through bosoms of threescore :—
  Draw near. The angels shall your introit sing,
  Fanning your weary foreheads with assuasive wing."

Again and again he loves to point out how with
benign solicitude the Church reconciles earth and
heaven :—

  " She plants a cross on every pine-girt ledge:
    A chancel by each river's lilied edge.
    Where'er her Catholic dominion broods,
    Behold how two Infinities are mated,
    The Mighty and Minute, by the control
    Of love or duty, linked with care sublime !
    On earth no spot, no fleeting point of time,
    Within our mind no thought, within our soul
    No feeling, doth she leave unconsecrated."

Just as Dr. Newman can think of England
only as the " Tyre of the West," so Mr. Aubrey de
Vere can think of her only as in the future a
penitent convert :—

  " It must be so. The sceptred hand whereon
    The secular future of the world is stayed

> Shall rise, its matricidal madness gone,
> Vestal once more. Once more, with saints to aid,
> England shall lift that conquering cross on high,
> Which gave her Constantine the victory."

Not long ago there died "A Priest of the Oratory," once well known and honoured in the English Church—Father Faber; and he, too, gave to the world, beside some purely spiritual works, a volume of poems. It might still be Mr. Aubrey de Vere who is writing, for the sentiment is the same; but it is not. It is Father Faber:

> " O France! all licence gained is but a loss
> Of liberty; and thou wert then most free
> When thou wert proud, with blameless pride, to be
> Nought but the foremost vassal of the Cross."

He speaks of the wide camp of angels :—

> " . . . . that essay
> Even now this glorious kingdom to recast
> With patient art in Faith's magnificent mould;
> To make it saintly as the France of old,
> And rivet once again its broken past."

When at Rome, Faber saw nothing but "Holy Church" warding off wrath from the world, and "weak saints upbearing thrones and states." Ages which are habitually spoken of with contempt are to him

> " Beautiful times, times past, in whose deep art,
>   As in a field by angels furrowed, lay
>   The seeds of heavenly beauty, set apart
>   For altar-flowers and ritual display.
>   Beautiful times, from whose calm bosom sprung
>   Abbeys and chantries, and a very host
>   Of quiet places upon every coast,
>   Where Christ was served, and blessed Mary sung."

In the sonnets on " Luther at Rome," " The Papacy," " Ordeals," etc., the same sentiments recur and abound, bringing into luminous distinction, to use his own phraseology,

> " The adverse circles of the Church and world."

About the same time that Faber died, died also Miss Adelaide Procter, who likewise was admitted some years before her death into the Roman Catholic Church; and her poems, written by her long before that event, are distinctly ominous of what was coming. She writes of

> " Crownëd Mind, and nothing more,
>   The great idol men adore."

Read her " Life and Death " :—

> " The crown must be won for Heaven, dear,
>   In the battle-field of life :
>   My child, though thy foes are strong and tried,
>   He loveth the weak and small;
>   The angels of Heaven are on thy side,
>   And God is over all."

Read her poem on " Thankfulness " :—

> " I thank Thee, Lord, that here our souls,
>   Though amply blest,
>   Can never find although they seek,
>   A perfect rest—
>   Nor ever shall, until they lean
>   On Jesus' breast."

Read her " Two Worlds," " The Warrior to his Dead Bride," " The Story of the Faithful Soul " —read, in fact, almost everything she has ever written—and you will find only pity for the world, a contempt of death, and a yearning, without any admixture of doubt, for the home beyond the grave :—

> " It is because my heart is stilled,
>   Not broken by despair,
>   Because I see the grave is bright,
>   And death itself is fair—
>   I dread no more the wrath of Heaven :
>   I have an angel there."

Far from dwelling too much, as some may possibly think I have done, on these Roman Catholic poets, I doubt if I have dwelt long enough. For I have by no means exhausted the list. The author of " The Angel in the House," Mr. Coventry Patmore, who had been writing in a

Roman Catholic strain years before he guessed it, has also now formally passed over to the Roman Catholic camp; and it will be interesting to compare his views upon woman—putting them side by side with those of Mr. Kenelm Digby, author of "Mores Catholici," etc., as recently expressed in a small volume of poetry, chiefly on that theme—with those held and expounded by the opposite poetical school of thought. Adding the remark that delicacy alone restrains me from naming one or two other fairly well-known poets and poetesses who seem to me to be on the highroad to Rome, I will close this portion of my subject.

But what are the literary reflections it suggests? Did these Roman Catholic poets stand alone, the phenomenon would still be remarkable enough. But they do not stand alone; and it is quite impossible that they should have done so. For they, too, form part of the Poetry of the Period; and if we had not such poems as the "In Memoriam" and "The Two Voices" of Mr. Tennyson, the "Christmas Eve and Easter Day" of Mr. Browning, "At the Grande Chartreuse" and "To the Memory of Obermann" by Mr. Arnold, the declared and defiant anti-Christian spirit of Mr. Swinburne, together with his glorification of paganism, in which he has been indirectly but practically joined by all the rest, neither should we have had "The Dream of Gerontius," and all the many various outpourings of a resolutely dogmatic Roman Catholic muse, such as we have been passing in review. For in addition to the other antics in which modern poetry indulges, it has positively taken upon itself to rush into controversy. An imaginary Cambridge mathematician has long been laughed at for asking what Milton's "Paradise Lost" proved. But a poem nowadays is almost as good as condemned if it proves nothing. Homer, Shakespeare, Dante, Chaucer, are all supposed, in this pottering, conscious nineteenth century, to have meant something more than lies on the surface; and hundreds of sapient expositors are busy telling us what is the inner meaning of their verse. What wonder, then, if poems written under the auspices of such a period should imbibe an argumentative temper, and poetry so far forget its mission as to set men by the ears and plunge them into the dismal vortex of contradictory demonstrations? It is wholly foreign to my purpose to inquire which of them is right. I hope I have shown, as far as opinion is concerned, the same toleration to Mr. Swinburne's Satyrs as to Dr. Newman's Angels, to Mr. Aubrey de Vere's and Father Faber's confident sonnets as to Mr. Tennyson's "faint trust in the larger hope," to Mr. Arnold's forlorn state of doubt as to Mr. Browning's invective against the "exhausted air-bell of the critic." The search after theological truths is not the province of the poet; and though passing allusions, such as are found in nearly all great poets, to the mysteries of life and death, are proper and reasonable enough, entire poems on the subject are as inappropriate as they are reprehensible. To indulge in them is only to drive one nail more into the coffin of the Poetry of the Period. And if such a search be forbidden to poets, *quâ* poets, equally forbidden must it be to the critic to ask what, in the way of truth, has come of their perverse inquiries. I have, therefore, rigidly abstained from asking. My function is something very different. It is to note that, whilst one set of poets are busy proclaiming that they believe everything, another that they believe a little, a third that they believe rather less, and a fourth that they believe nothing at all, the cause of sincere faith or of sincere scepticism is not advanced one jot, and the cause, end, and aim of poetry are being forgotten altogether. I have already said that Science is an intruder inside the domains of the Muse. Theology has just as little right to admittance. And it is only in an age in which the Muse is incapable of holding its own, by producing really great poetry, that such a monstrous confusion of limits and functions could possibly have occurred.

The Poetry of the Future.

MANY people will, I daresay, be surprised to find that the Poetry of the Period is not yet exhausted, and still more astonished at the "Poetry of the Future" being placed in that category. But have they not heard of the "Music of the Future;" and not only heard of it, but heard it? It is not a thing promised, but a thing accomplished. The foundations of it at least are laid; and even these are pronounced by its prophets to be already superior to the highest summits ever attained by such puny composers of the past as Mozart, Handel, and Beethoven. So is it with the Poetry of the Future. It consists of no merely prophesied strains: the first singer of it is here and amongst us, and his previous productions are to be had at the circulating libraries.

True, he is only the first of a long succession of coming bards; but these will follow in his footsteps, as Virgil is said to have trodden in those of Homer, Dante in those of Virgil, Milton in those of Dante, and so on through the sustained inheritance of song. If, as has been seen, we are not overwell satisfied with such productions of the muse as are vouchsafed us by living English bards, we have no reason to distress ourselves, or even to cast fond eyes upon the bygone days of a happier poetical literature, in order to find consolation. We must look forwards, not backwards. Not Byron and his predecessors, but Mr. Walt Whitman and his successors, constitute the balm that still abides in Gilead. The Old World is done up, no doubt; but Apollo has taken refuge in the United States. The pottering little fountain of Hippocrene, now run dry, has been replaced by the tremendous waters of the everlasting Mississippi, and the Parnassian and Heliconian ranges have abdicated in favour of the Alleghanies and the setting sun.

That my readers may not think I am setting up imaginary claims, I must beg to be permitted to lay before them the proofs of their existence; and I have less scruple in doing so, as I fancy I have in store for them no mean entertainment. To some of them the name of Mr. Walt Whitman will be faintly familiar; but to others, and indeed the majority, I imagine it will represent nothing at all. It is highly desirable that they should become more intimately acquainted with a gentleman who, both through his own voice, and (as we shall shortly see) through the voices of some exceedingly well-known English admirers, affects to be doing so much for the present and future literary greatness of the human race.

Mr. Walt Whitman was incited to compose the various poems from which copious citations will be made as we proceed, by a contempt for the Poetry of the Period; and it is obvious that he, therefore, has a special claim upon our attention. His opinion of it is, that it is either "the poetry of an elegantly weak sentimentalism, at bottom nothing but maudlin puerilities, or more or less musical verbiage, arising out of a life of depression and enervation as their result; or else that class ·of poetry, plays, etc., of which the foundation is feudalism, with its ideas of lords and ladies, its standard of gentility, and the manners of high life below stairs in every line and verse." From him we are to expect no such

feminine and frivolous stuff; he is as masculine
—again another reason for our examining his
pretensions—as any of us, sick of the feminine
twang of other lyres, can possibly desire :—

" No dainty dolcè affetuoso I;
   Branded, sunburnt, grey-necked, forbidding, I have
      arrived,
   To be wrestled with as I pass, for the solid prizes of
      the universe."

He is declared by one of his most ardent
admirers, Mr. W. M. Rossetti—to whom I shall
have to revert more than once in this paper,
and who is esteemed, by a select but somewhat
notorious circle, a mighty authority in poetical
matters—to " occupy at the present moment a
unique position on the globe, and one which,
even in past times, can have been occupied by
only an infinitesimally small number of men. He
is the one man who entertains and professes
respecting himself the grave conviction, that he
is the actual and prospective founder of a new
poetic literature, and a great one—a literature
proportional to the material vastness and the
unmeasured destinies of America. He believes
that the Columbus of the Continent, or the
Washington of the States, was not more truly

than himself the patron and founder and up-builder of this America."

That this is no exaggerated account of Mr. Walt Whitman's estimate of himself is apparent on almost every page of his writings, for on page after page it is distinctly laid down :—

" See, projected through time,
　For me an audience interminable.
　Successions of men, Americanos, a hundred millions;
　With faces turned sideways or backward towards me,
　　　to listen,
　With eyes retrospective towards Me."

" Americanos ! conquerors ! marches humanitarian ;
　Foremost ! century marches !　Libertad ! masses !
　For you a programme of chants !"

" In the year 80 of the States,
　My tongue, every atom of my blood, formed from this
　　　soil, this air,
　Born here of parents born here, from parents the same,
　　　and their parents the same,
　I, now thirty-six old, in perfect health begin,
　Hoping to cease not till death."

At another time he exclaims :—

" For your life, adhere to me ;
　Of all men of the earth, I only can unloose you and
　　　toughen you.
　None have understood you, but I understand you.
　I have the idea of all, and am all, and believe in all.
　Within me latitude widens, longitude lengthens."

It will very likely be objected, that though, perhaps, no such wonderful phenomenon has previously been witnessed as a person believing that within him has taken place so supernatural an operation as the one intimated in the above concluding line, yet the world has seen a goodly number of individuals who proclaimed themselves to be the coming man; and that the estimate formed by Mr. Walt Whitman of himself, is no test of the estimate other people form of him. Let us then come to that; for, after all, that is the most wonderful as it is the most important part of the affair. And, to begin with, let us see what is thought of this poetical avatar by Mr. Rossetti; cramming (for brevity's sake) into one paragraph the diffuse eulogies which this gentleman has passed upon him :—

Mr. Whitman's poem, he says, "is, *par excellence,* the modern poem. . . . It forms incomparably the *largest* performance of our period in poetry. . . . He breaks with all precedent. . . . His work is practically certain to stand as archetypal for many future poetic efforts. The entire book may be called the pæan of the natural man. . . . This most remarkable poet is the founder of *American* poetry, rightly to be called,

and the most sonorous poetic voice of the tangi-
bilities of actual and prospective democracy. . . .
If anything can cast, in the eyes of posterity, an
added halo of brightness round the unsullied
personal qualities and the great doings of Lincoln,
it will assuredly be the written monument reared
to him by Whitman. I sincerely believe him to
be of the order of *great* poets, and by no means
of pretty good ones. . . . I believe that Whitman is one of the huge, as yet mainly unrecog-
nized, forces of our time—privileged to evoke,
in a country hitherto still asking for its poet, a
fresh, athletic, and American poetry, and pre-
destined to be traced up to by generation after
generation of believing and ardent disciples.
. . . . Poets, said Shelley, are the unacknowledged legislators of mankind. Whitman seems
in a peculiar degree marked out for legislation of
the kind referred to. His voice will one day be
potential or magisterial wherever the English
language is, spoken—that is to say, in the four
corners of the earth; and in his own American
hemisphere, the uttermost avatars of democracy
will confess him not more their announcer than
their inspirer."

I think that, after these samples of Mr.

Rossetti's opinion as to Mr. Walt Whitman, it
will be confessed I have not begun by exaggerating his pretensions as acknowledged in certain
quarters. Mr. Rossetti has given utterance to
his views in the columns of highly influential
critical journals; and his views .plainly are, that
Mr. Whitman is the Homer of the New World,
and that his " Leaves of Grass" and " Drum
Taps" will be regarded by " Americanos" to
come with the same love and veneration with
which European men of letters 'regard the Iliad
and the Odyssey.

Another of the admirers of this " unacknowledged legislator" is Mr. Robert Buchanan, himself by profession both a poet and a critic. Mr.
Buchanan's opinions on the subject are embodied
in a paper published some little time back in
the " Broadway"; and though he does not like to
talk of his author as an artist, and sees plainly
enough that he is obviously deficient in certain
qualities which have hitherto been deemed indispensable in a poet, he has formed an estimate
not much less flattering than Mr. Rossetti's. I
will apply to it the same method of compression
which has been already employed in the case of
the latter : —

" Walt Whitman," writes Mr. Buchanan, is already exercising on the youth of America an influence similar to that exercised by Socrates over the youth of Greece, or by Raleigh over the young chivalry of England. In a word, he has become a *sacer- vates*—his ministry is admitted by palpable live disciples. . . . . We are in concert with those who believe his to be a genuine ministry, large in its spiritual manifestations, and abundant in capabilities for good. . . . . He professes to sow the first seeds of an indigenous literature, by putting in music the spiritual and fleshly yearnings of the cosmical man. . . . . He sees in the American future the grandest realization of centuries of idealism. . . . . Thoughts crowd so thick upon him that he has no time to seek their artistic equivalent ;* he utters his thoughts in any way, and his expressions gain accidental beauty from the glamour of his sympathy. . . . . He is inspired. . . . .

* As if poetical thoughts did not always bring their artistic equivalent with them !—the thought and the form, or expression, being one. Mr. Buchanan is evidently just as much at sea as are most of his contemporaries as to the genesis of poetry, and just as little aware that poetry, like the poet, is born, not made. Does he suppose Shakespeare went " *seeking* " for " artistic equivalents" ?

In actual living force, in grip and muscle, he
has no equal among contemporaries. . . . . He
is the voice of which America stood most in
need. . . . . He is the clear forerunner of the
great American poet, long longed for, often
prophesied."

This, in substance, is Mr. Buchanan's conclusion. But Mr. Rossetti, besides favouring us
with his own opinion on the subject, is good
enough to inform us of various other critical
authorities who are pretty much of his way of
thinking. Amongst these he names Mr. William
Bell Scott, a name, perhaps, not very familiar to
most of my readers, but which Mr. Rossetti
answers for as belonging to "a true poet and a
strong thinker"; and Mr. Scott, he says, considers that the value of Mr. Whitman's poetry
is real and great. The name of Mr. Swinburne,
however, is known far and wide; and Mr. Rossetti informs us that " he also is an ardent admirer
of Whitman." Of English newspapers which
have paid him a proper tribute, he mentions the
" Dispatch," the " Leader," the " London Review," and the " Pall Mall Gazette." I have not
seen the notices referred to, but am quite willing
to take Mr. Rossetti's word for it that the journals

in question have shown themselves "discerning" in
the matter. What meaning Mr. Rossetti attaches
to " discernment," in estimating Mr. Whitman's
literary merits and position—unless, indeed, he
would allow that his own estimate is very undis-
cerning—we have already seen ; and though we
may be surprised to hear that a journal so little
disposed to deal in extravagances on its own
account, or to welcome them in others, as the
" Pall Mall Gazette," has been " discerning "
towards Mr. Walt Whitman in Mr. Rossetti's
sense, I suppose it is so. After naming various
other literary authorities, who, he says, " express
themselves with no measured enthusiasm," and
referring to an anonymous critic, " highly entitled
to form an opinion on any poetic question, whose
admiration and enjoyment of Whitman's greatness grow keener and warmer every time he
thinks of him," Mr. Rossetti crowns his array of
flattering testimonies by appealing to Mr. Emer-
son. The opinion of the latter gentleman is that
" ' Leaves of Grass ' is the most extraordinary
piece of wit and wisdom that America has yet
contributed."

So much for what are called critical opinions.
Some people, however, opine that the proof of a

poem is in the selling; but here, again, Mr. Walt Whitman's admirers may fairly claim to be able to produce satisfactory evidence. The first edition of "Leaves of Grass," consisting of about a thousand copies, was sold off in less than a year. A second edition excited, we are told, "a considerable storm," and a further edition, now of between four and five thousand copies, followed. Other editions have since been issued.

It is perfectly clear, therefore, that, whether we appeal to the judgment of individuals supposed to be possessed of due literary qualifications, or to the great American public, we must accept it as a fact that we are pressingly invited to recognize Mr. Walt Whitman as "the founder of American poetry," rightly to be called, "as one of the order of great poets," as "one of the huge forces of our time," as an "unacknowledged legislator," as a voice "potential or magisterial wherever the English language is spoken," as "the announcer and inspirer of the uttermost avatars of democracy"—in a word, as the founder of the Poetry of the Future.

Such being the case, let us boldly look this bold man in the face, and see what he is like; for if he really be not only of the order of great poets, but the founder of an absolutely new school of poetry, evidently he is a pearl beyond all price. His fundamental notions of poetry are, I must confess, for the most part correct. "The direct trial of him," he says in his preface to "Leaves of Grass," "who would be the greatest poet, is to-day. As if it were necessary to trot back generation after generation to the Eastern records!" I have myself so strongly insisted on this point, that I need scarcely say I cordially agree with the sentiments thus expressed. The trial of the great poet is undoubtedly to-day. I, however, have asserted in no doubtful terms that the trial is too great, and that to-day has produced and can produce no great poet. Mr. Whitman says it can and has, and he is the great poet it has produced. The present age has broken with the past, and he has done the same; and he is the great poet of to-day, and the founder of the great Poetry of the Future.

> " See projected through time,
> For me an audience interminable."

> " Whoever you are! to you endless announcements."

> " Daughter of the lands, did you wait for your poets?
> Did you wait for one with a flowing mouth and
> indicative hand?"

"Toward the male of the States, and toward the
    female of the States,
Give words—words to the lands."

" Still the present I raise aloft—still the future of the
    States I harbinge, glad and sublime."

Mr. Whitman then sings of to-day, and does
so of set purpose—a purpose with which I should
heartily sympathize if I did not feel the profound
conviction that doing so is only lost time. The
next question is, What does he see in to-day to
sing? He sees four things: namely, America,
Democracy, Personality, and Materialism. These
for him are the subjects of song both in the
present and the future; and he would be a bold
man who would deny that, if to-day be the trial
of a great poet, these four things may, if not
must, properly constitute the great poet's themes.
Let us see what he has to say concerning each of
them in succession.

The references to America—its greatness, bigness, wonderfulness—in Mr. Whitman's " Poems"
are incessant; and certainly the glory of one's
country has ever been deemed a worthy subject
for the muse :—

" Successions of men, Americanos, a hundred millions,
    For you a programme of chants.

> Chants of the prairies;
> Chants of the long-running Mississippi, and down to
> the Mexican sea;
> Chants of Ohio, Indiana, Illinois, Iowa, Wisconsin,
> and Minnesota;
> Chants going forth from the centre, from Kansas,
> and thence equi-distant,
> Shooting in pulses of fire, ceaseless, to vivify all."

> " Take my leaves, America! take them South, and
> take them North!
> Surround them, East and West! for they would
> surround you."

> " I will report all heroism from an American point of
> view."

> " America always!
> Always our own feuillage.
> Always Florida's green peninsula! Always the
> priceless delta of Louisiana! Always the cotton-
> fields of Alabama and Texas !
> Always," etc.

And so on, through pages of what Mr. Rossetti calls " the first order of poetry." I need scarcely load my pages with quotations from well-known poets on the subject of their country, but may rest content with saying that, if the foregoing be poetry at all, all that Virgil, Horace, Ovid, and Lucan have written about Rome—all that Dante, Petrarch, Tasso, and Alfieri have written about Italy—all that Scott and Burns have written about Scotland—had better be flung into the dusthole and forgotten. In his preface to "Leaves of Grass," Mr. Whitman informs us that "the United States themselves are essentially the greatest poem;" and farther on, in the same production, he declares that "of all nations, the United States, with veins full of poetical stuff, will doubtless have the greatest poets"—he himself being, as we have seen, the forerunner and first of them. All this, as anybody can perceive who possesses an atom of penetration, arises simply from Mr. Whitman's admiration of bigness—which he mistakes for greatness—attempting to carry it on his shoulders, and staggering under it most woefully. In fact, all the quotations as yet made from his "poems"—and so far I have quoted only the most rational of them—will, I fancy, strike the reader as resembling more what they will imagine must have been the improvising of savages in their literary moods before (if the bull may be pardoned) letters were known at all.

> "O Camerado close!
> O you and me at last—and us two only!
> O a word to clear one's path ahead endlessly!
> *O something ecstatic and undemonstrable! O music
> wild!*"

> "All these States compact—every square mile of
>   these States without excepting a particle.
> O land! O all so dear to me--what you are (wherever
>   it is), I become a part of that, whatever it is!
> Southward, then, I go screaming, with wings slowly
>   flapping, with the myriad of gulls wintering
>   along the coasts of Florida."

I confess I think the picture not an inaccurate
one. Mr. Walt Whitman screaming, and with
wings slowly flapping, realizes my notion of
him in his poetical condition—this Gull of
Mississippi, as opposed to the Swan of Avon—
as perfectly as language could well present it
to us.

In connection with this wild inarticulate worship of America must be noticed Mr. Whitman's
attempts at what may be called Universality. It
is one of the tricks of our time, and, as a matter
of course, he is infected with it. Unable, just
like many of his somewhat less boisterous contemporaries, to understand the vast problem presented by the past, present, and future of the
world, like them again he fancies he has solved
it by a clumsy application of the *Bene quodcunque
est* doctrine. Here is his way of expressing himself on the subject:

"I respect Assyria, China, Teutonia, and the Hebrews;
  I adopt each theory, myth, god, and demigod;
  I see that the old accounts, Bibles, genealogies, are true
      without exception.
  I assert that all past days were what they should have
      been,
  And that they could nohow have been better than they
      were;
  And that to-day is what it should be, and that America is,
  And that to-day and America could nohow be better
      than they are."

It is just possible that some people will find this assuring; but I should vastly like to see the person who thinks it poetry, let alone of "the highest order of poetry." In one of his "poems," called "Salut Au Monde," he gets hold of the atlas, enumerates nearly every spot on the face of the globe, and says that he sees, hears, and belongs to it. It is done in this fashion:—

"I see the cities of the earth, and make myself at random
      a part of them;
I am a real Parisian;
I am a habitant of Vienna, St. Petersburg, Berlin,
      Constantinople;
I am of Adelaide, Sydney, Melbourne;
I am of London, Manchester, Bristol, Edinburgh,
      Limerick;
I am of Madrid, Cadiz, Barcelona, Oporto, Lyons, Brussels,
      Berne, Frankfort, Stuttgart, Turin, and Florence."

And so on, varied by "I see," "I hear," "I behold." But he goes still farther than this. His "Universality" embraces not only all places, but all persons, and everything they can do, good, bad, or indifferent :—

> "Good or bad, I never question—I love all—I do not
>   condemn anything ;
> To me detected persons are not, in any respect, worse
>   than undetected persons—and are not in any
>   respect worse than I am myself.
> To me any judge, or any juror, is equally criminal with
>   criminals—and any reputable person is also—and
>   the President is also."

> "Omnes! Omnes! let others ignore what they may ;
> I make the poem of evil also—I commemorate that part
>   also ;
> I am myself just as much evil as good, and my nation is—
> And I say there is in fact no evil ;
> Or, if there is, I say it is just as important to you, to
>   the land, or to me, as anything else."

There is much more to the same effect which cannot possibly be quoted ; but when I add that he avers ugliness to be as welcome to him as beauty, and declares, on one occasion, " I will sleep with the cleaners of ——" (there is no blank in the original), a fair notion of Mr. Whitman's poetical universality—springing from and invariably returning to the central notion that everything either is America or has been made for it—will have been obtained by the reader.

America thus being the very stock-in-trade of his compositions, Democracy, as a matter of course, comes in for considerable glorification, after the author's tumultuous fashion :—

" Democracy !
  Near at hand to you a throat is now inflating itself and
      joyfully singing !
  Ma femme !
  For the brood beyond us and of us !
  For those who belong here, and those to come,
  I exultant, to be ready for them, will now shake out
      carols stronger and haughtier than have ever yet
      been heard upon earth."

A story is told of a countryman of Mr. Walt Whitman, who, after reading Mr. Tennyson's " In Memoriam," passed on it the not inapt criticism, " What on airth is the use of screaming against the calm facts of creation ?" Mr. Whitman evidently thinks that, at any rate, there is a good deal of use in screaming *for* them. He wishes to see Democracy screaming too :—

> "Thunder on! stride on, Democracy! strike with
> 	vengeful stroke!
> And do you rise higher than ever yet, O days, O cities!
> Crash heavier, heavier yet, O storms! you have done
> 	me good!"

Borne almost beyond himself, he in one place
exclaims :—

> "Bully for you! you proud, friendly, free Manhattanese!"

But, of course, all Americans are equally proud,
friendly, and free, and every one of them is just
as proud, friendly, free, and everything else, as
every other :—

> "The wife—and she is not one jot less that the husband;
> The daughter—and she is just as good as the son;
> The mother—and she is every bit as much as the father."

One more quotation, and we will leave this
second theme of Mr. Walt Whitman's :—

> "I sing the Equalities,
> I sing the Finale of things.
> I announce natural persons to arise.
> I announce uncompromising liberty and equality.
> I announce splendours and majesties to make all the
> 	previous politics of the earth insignificant."

His glorification of the individual, or Personality, as he himself loves to call it, is nearly

as frequent, and to the full as conspicuous. He never alludes to subordination or co-ordination; he knows them not. The doctrine of Pope, that :—

> " Order is Heaven's first law; and, that confessed,
>   Some are and must be better than the rest;"

and that of Shakespeare :—

> " Take but degree away, untune that string,
>   And mark what discord follows"—

are unknown to him; or, if they are known, he utterly contemns them. As he says, he sings the Equalities, with a large E.

> " I will effuse egotism, and show it underlying all—and
>   I will be the bard of personality."

Sometimes he glorifies it in himself, sometimes in another, sometimes in himself and another together :—

> " Rest not, till you rivet and publish yourself of your
>   own Personality.
>   Go, mon cher! if need be, and inure yourself to self-
>   esteem—elevatedness."

> " I celebrate myself,
>   And what I assume you shall assume,
>   For every atom belonging to me, as good belongs to
>   you."

"O my comrade!
  O you and me at last, and us two only!
  O to level occupations and the sexes! O to bring all
      to common ground! O adhesiveness!
  O the pensive aching to be together—you know not
      why, and I know not why."

" Who need be afraid of the merge?
  Undrape! you are not guilty to me, nor stale, nor
      discarded;
  I see through the broadcloth and gingham, whether or
      no."

" Me imperturbe,
  Me standing at ease in Nature,
  Master of all—aplomb in the midst of irrational things,
  Me private or public (I am eternally equal with the
      best—I am not subordinate)."

And, as a matter of course, You doing the same
thing, and occupying the same proud position!

We now arrive at the fourth of the main
themes whose glories Mr. Walt Whitman and his
admirers consider that he is specially commissioned to sing, or (as he himself expresses it)
to "yawp over the roofs of the world." I mean
—Materialism. We are informed, by one of the
many curiositymongers who have busied themselves with Mr. Whitman's private habits—with
which we have nothing to do—that he is exceed-

ingly communicative on all subjects save one. If
interrogated as to his theological opinions, he
turns dead silent. In his compositions, however,
he is garrulous enough upon the subject, and
some will think rather contradictory. He speaks
continually of the Soul; but then there is, I
should imagine, no word in the language capable
of a vague signification, and of being commenced
with a capital, that does not find its way into his
tumultuous tossing-together of the component
parts of the dictionary. How far he understands
the Soul in any recognized acceptation of the
word, my readers will judge for themselves, when
they have seen a few of his utterances on the
subject :—

> " Was somebody asking to see the Soul?
>> See! your own shape and countenance—persons, sub-
>>> stances, beasts, the trees, the running rivers, the
>>> rocks, and sands!
>> How can the real body ever die and be buried?
>> Behold! the body includes and is the meaning, the
>>> main concern—and includes and is the soul.
>> Whoever you are! how superb and how divine is your
>>> body, or any part of it!"

With him this is a rooted conviction. He
says that he is " divine inside and out," and with
a licence of language—which is a mere nothing

to what he often indulges in, but which in this instance makes us lose our sense of profanity in an irresistible peal of laughter—he assures us that "the scent of these armpits is an aroma finer than prayer!" If he worships any particular thing, he says it shall be "some of the spread of my own body." One long passage commences thus :—

"O my body! I dare not desert the likes of you in either
        men or women, nor the likes of the parts of you;
I believe the likes of you are to stand or fall with the
        likes of the Soul (and that they are the Soul).
Head, neck, hair, ears, drop and tympan of the ears,
Nose, nostrils of the nose, and the partition,
Cheeks, temples, forehead, chin, throat, back of the
        neck, neck slue,
Upper arm, armpit, elbow-socket, lower arm, arm-
        sinews, arm-bones,
Ribs, belly, backbone, joints of the backbone,
The thin red jellies within you, or with me—
O, I say now, these are not the parts and poems of the
        body only, but of the Soul!
O, I say these are the Soul!"

It must not be supposed that I have quoted the entire passage. I dare not. Suffice it to say that the enumeration covers two long pages, and that, physiologically speaking, it is exhaustive. Nor is his admiration confined to the human body :—

> "Beef in the butcher's stall, the area of pens of live pork,
>   the killing-hammer, the hog-hook, the scalder's
>   tub, gutting, the gutter's cleaver, the packer's
>   maul, and the plenteous winter-work of pork-
>   packing,
> In them poems for you and me.
> I say that none lead to greater than those lead to."

As a concluding and crowning embodiment and expression of Mr. Whitman's Materialism, let us take the following :—

> "I will make the poems of materials, for I think these
>   are to be the most spiritual poems,
> And I will make the poems of my body and of mor-
>   tality.
> For I shall then supply myself with the poems of the
>   Soul, and of immortality.
> Strange and hard that paradox true I give ;
> Objects gross and the unseen Soul are one."

I trust no one has supposed that, in giving extracts from Mr. Walt Whitman's " poems," as far as they relate to America, Democracy, Personality, and Materialism, I have been intending to turn his opinions into ridicule, or even to quarrel with him in the least for holding them. I need scarcely say, that his opinions are not mine, but neither are those of Mr. Swinburne or Doctor Newman; yet I believe it will be allowed that I attempted to cast no slur on the opinions of either of those writers. That is not the function of the purely literary critic. Mr. Whitman is as heartily welcome to his views of the Universe, as far as I am concerned, as anybody else is: and if I have brought them into prominence, it is only because I thought that the account of him would thus be made both more entertaining and more complete; whilst at the same time I should be compelled to make quotations from him with obvious impartiality, and the reader would obtain just as fair an idea of his literary merits as if I had proceeded in a less methodical fashion.

Mr. Whitman's opinions, therefore, be his own, without any controversy! But I do not think I should be doing my duty if I did not inform the reader, who may possibly have been just a little offended by certain of the passages I have cited, that his "poems" swarm with pages upon pages of whose horrible and ineffable nastiness they cannot possibly form any conception. Mr. Rossetti—who is the editor of the English edition, and who has omitted from it the parts to which I chiefly refer—considers that most of them would be better away, and doubts whether even one of them deserves to be retained in the exact phraseology it at present exhibits. I wish Mr. Rossetti had contented himself with this avowal, quite insufficient under the circumstances as I think it. Unfortunately, he has balanced this mild reprobation by the averment, in another place, that he has excluded the "poems" to which I refer, out of deference to "the propriety of the peculiarly nervous age," and that he "sacrifices them grudgingly." I think I have shown myself not particularly squeamish; but if I were myself to print the very least offensive of the passages alluded to—though they circulate freely in America—I should very justly be greeted with a storm of reprobation.

Anybody who considers the matter will see that this has a direct bearing on the purely literary side of the question. Mr. Whitman over and over again protests that he has no shame. As Mr. Buchanan—mildly even—puts it for him, " He sees that the beasts are not ashamed; why, therefore, should he be ashamed?" Here we have it. He recognizes no shame, no law, no forms, no good, no evil, no beauty, no ugliness, no distinctions, differences, or limitations. This, of course, will account for the disconnectedness of his utterances, and the utter disorder of his language. I suspect that many readers will here be inclined to say, what doubtless they have long been thinking—" What is the use of proving the self-evident, that all which Mr. Walt Whitman writes is stark staring nonsense, both in substance and in form equally ?" I can fully sympathize with the impatience which prompts such an interruption ; but whilst doing so, I would ask them to turn once again to the encomiums, passed by others upon these productions, which were cited at starting in order to preclude the notion that I was wasting powder. With regard to the form of Mr. Whitman's compositions, I would ask them to attend for a moment to what Mr. Rossetti and Mr. Buchanan, let alone others equally pretending to authority, have to say on this particular point.

" Whitman's poems," writes the former, " present no trace of rhyme save in a couple or so of chance instances. Parts of them, indeed, may be regarded as a warp of prose amid the weft of poetry, such as Shakespeare furnishes the precedent for in drama. Still there is a very powerful and majestic rhythmical sense through-out."

Mr. Buchanan, as we have seen, writes with much more moderation than Mr. Rossetti; but even he asserts that Mr. Whitman's language is " strong, vehement, always forcible, and some-times even rhythmical, like the prose of Plato ; " that his lines are " lines of unrhymed verse, very Biblical in form, and showing indeed on every page the traces of Biblical influence ; " and that he has " risen on the States to point the way to new literatures."

Such, then, being the opinions which, it must be presumed, some people in these strange days entertain, since they express them, of Mr. Walt Whitman's literary claims, I think it right, if only to liberate my soul—and I should imagine those of most of my readers—emphatically, but in all serious calmness, to declare, on the contrary, my opinion, that his style has nothing in common with either the Bible, Shakespeare, Plato, or any other hitherto honoured name in literature ; but that his grotesque, ungrammatical, and repulsive rhapsodies can be fitly compared only to the painful ravings of maniacs' dens.

Such, however, is the Poetry of the Future ?

Perhaps it is. If so, we must console ourselves by reflecting that, unsatisfactory as may be the Poetry of the Period, if we had been born a generation later still, our poetical plight would have been yet worse than it is. Yet I shrewdly suspect that one is the child of the other. Mr. Whitman himself distinctly says that it is. As I have already stated, he informs us that he was urged to lay the foundations of the Poetry of the Future, because, in his opinion, that of the Period is " the poetry of an elegantly weak sentimentalism, at bottom nothing but maudlin puerilities, or more or less musical verbiage"—in a word, because, as I have been urging in those essays, it is deficient in all masculine and lofty qualities. Mr. Whitman revolts against it ; and his is a revolt with a vengeance. Mr. Tennyson and his admirers have been fancying that they had swept and garnished the Halls of Literature, got rid of all such objectionable robustness as figures in the verse of a Shakespeare, a Byron, or a Burns, and made the place sweet, trim, and pretty for all time.   But, alas ! seven devils worse than the first have entered, and its state promises to be more terrible than ever.   Nor do I feel sure that there is not a good deal of truth in what Mr.

Whitman says of the same school of poetry being based on a now extinct feudalism, and on standards of gentility belonging to a somewhat later period. At any rate, he will have none of these. As Mr. Rossetti reminds us, it has been said of Mr. Whitman by one of his warmest admirers, "He is Democracy." I really think he is—in his compositions, at least; being, like it, ignorant, sanguine, noisy, coarse, and chaotic! Democracy may be, and I fear is, our proximate future; and it will, as a matter of course, bring its poetry along with it. The prospect is not an agreeable one; but, as a protection both against it and our present condition, we can always fall back upon the grand old masters of the Past, from whom it is quite certain that singers, whether insipid or insane, will never succeed in weaning the healthy opinion of mankind.

Supernatural Poetry.

I PROPOSE, in this chapter, to present the reader with an account of certain poems, which, unless their alleged origin can be proved to be an imposture, must be regarded as perhaps the most remarkable phenomena of modern times. Were the poems worthless in themselves, or even of a mediocre order, it would perhaps scarcely be worth while in these pages to call attention to the peculiar circumstances under which they profess to have been composed. Even, however, if we end by denying them the spiritual character they claim, they are, as I think the reader will acknowledge, sufficiently meritorious, from a literary point of view, to demand our notice. How strongly entitled, then, must they be to prominent mention, if, in addition to their poetical deserts, their supernatural birth can be established! On this latter point I am unable to arrive at a confident decision. In which direction my opinion inclines will be manifest as we go along, and likewise the reasons for remaining at the end, in a state of partial doubt.

The coarser phenomena of what is best known by the name of Spiritualism must be more or less familiar to the majority of my readers; but perhaps not quite so many of them are aware that these present little, if any, absolute novelty. Planchette has been known in China for hundreds, probably for thousands, of years; vision-yielding balls of crystal are familiar to all who are acquainted with Arabian literature; and a crystal ball has, from time immemorial, been one of the three symbols of sovereignty associated with the Emperor of Japan. Some persons have seen in the Delphic tripod from which the Pythian priestess delivered her oracles—and which has its analogue in Thor's Kettle (probably the origin of the witches' cauldron)—an anticipation of modern table-turning; and in the Babylonian, Libyan, Delphian, Cimmerian, Erythræan, Samian, Cumæan (probably the same as the Erythræan), Trojan, Phrygian, Tiburtine, early

Christian, and other less well-recognized Sibyls, it is not surprising if people see the fore-runners of the reputed seers, seeresses, and mediums of to-day. These, however, have little in common with the extra-terrestrial utterances with which I have now to deal. It is true that some of the Sibyls must have been remarkably communicative, if, as we are told, more than two thousand of their books were consumed by the order of Augustus, when, at the inauguration of the Empire, he feared lest those which existed in private hands should be turned to hostile political purposes. It is true, likewise, that several of the Oracles responded in a human voice and in human language, and professed to be moved by a divine afflatus, as in the orgasms of the Pythia; the oracular responses, moreover, being occasionally delivered in verse. But when we had exhausted all that might be said upon the subject, we should still fall far short of a parallel or anticipation to the modern phenomenon to which I will now at once betake myself—the delivery of volumes of verse of an undeniably excellent sort, by persons professing to be in a spiritual trance, to be mere instruments played on by invisible singers—some of the latter unknown to them even by name—others known to them as but recently rid of the flesh—others, again, being the spirits of departed bards of varying fame, commencing with Shakespeare and ending with Pollok!

The first author of this class to whom I would call attention is Mr. Thomas Lake Harris, of whose personal history I will give a brief sketch, as soon as I have succeeded in interesting my readers in him by making them acquainted with his "Poems." These, as far as I know them, consist of "A Lyric of the Golden Age," "An Epic of the Starry Heaven," "A Lyric of the Morning Land," "Regina, a Song of Many Days," and a volume of "Hymns of Spiritual Devotion." I shall, perhaps, best introduce them by quoting at once some of the opening lines of "A Lyric of the Morning Land," which profess to narrate its origin and history :—

> " This poem is a love-child of the skies.
>   *   *   *   *   *
> When the last rose was breathing life away,
> It sprang to outward shape; unformed by art,
> Full-fledged it left its nest within the heart,
> And sang melodious in external airs.
> As the same rose-tree many roses bears,
> As the same eye hath many smiles of light,

And the same bosom many a sweet delight,
And the same lute a manifold refrain,
And many drops one golden shower of rain:
So the same heaven from whence this child came
    down,
Peopled by deathless ones of old renown,
Hath many poems mightier and more grand
Than this fair infant from the Morning Land.

"When summer clouds went wandering o'er the streams,
    Our Medium sang it, whilst entranced in dreams,
    Through twilight and sweet morn. A faithful friend,
    The rapid speech, trance-spoken, truly penned;
    And all the while the Spirit, through whose breath
    The song was uttered, knew terrestrial death,
    And, in his inmost, felt, saw, heard, and knew
    The bright song's essence. . . . .
    And for the rest, 'twas given, as one might play
    Upon a lute, at intervals by day,
    Within the space it takes the moon t' unfold
    Her slender crescent to a disc of gold;
    And 'twere not hard to count the time in hours—
    Ten full-blown roses, twenty orange-flowers."

In an Appendix may be found a prose account of the history of the poem, which tallies with the foregoing, but the substance of which I will give, in order to make the sense of the latter clear beyond the possibility of misconception. It is, in effect, that in January, 1854, at the hour of noon, Mr. Harris passed into a spiritual or interior condition, the archetypal ideas which the poem

developes being inwrought by spiritual agency
into his inmost mind. It was not, however, till
August of the same year, that, having attained
their maturity, they descended into the externals
of his mind, uttered themselves in speech, and
were transcribed as spoken by the Medium, Mr.
Harris himself: he, by spiritual agencies, being
temporarily elevated to the spiritual degree of
the mind necessary for that purpose, and the
external form being rendered quiet by a process
which is analogous to physical death. The poem
was dictated, at intervals, during parts of fourteen
days, the actual time occupied by its delivery being
about thirty hours, or, as it is poetically said :—

> " Within the space it takes the moon t' unfold
> Her slender crescent to a disc of gold ;
> And 'twere not hard to count the time in hours—
> Ten full-blown roses, twenty orange-flowers."

I cannot pretend to unfold here the " archetypal ideas" spoken of. Those who are curious
in the matter must read the whole poem itself;
and it will repay perusal. Suffice it me, on that
score, to say that here, as elsewhere in Mr.
Harris's poems, the influence of Swedenborg's
ideas is as apparent as is that of Shelley's literary
style; Mr. Harris professing, in one of his prose

works, to have had interviews with the former well-known and illustrious personage. For the rest, since I have yet so much to say on the subject, I must confine myself to a few extracts from "A Lyric of the Morning Land," in order to justify my good opinion of its poetical merits. The following passage is quoted, not on account of its exceptional excellence, but as bearing directly on the objection, so often and so naturally made, to the preference of Spiritualists for night, or darkness, in which to produce their phenomena :—

> " The spiritual ministry of night
> 　　Is all unknown.　Day rules the sensuous mind ;
> 　　But night the fettered spirit doth unbind,
> And through the silver palace-gates of light,
> 　　In dream and trance she bears the soul away
> 　　To the wide landscape of the inner day.
> 　　　*　　*　　*　　*　　*
>
> The souls of men are wanderers while they sleep ;
> 　　And life's continuous current ever flows,
> Whether to outward bliss the pulses leap,
> 　　Or languid glide in silence and repose.
> 　　　*　　*　　*　　*　　*
>
> The charmed islands of the Asteroids
> 　　Are nearer far than Ceylon or Cathay ;
> For angel hosts, who throng the seeming voids
> 　　Of visible space, the human heart survey,
> And wear meanwhile such blessed spells, that they

> Touch with their subtle sense the inner mind,
> And all the fettered inner wings unbind,
> Till we rise at their call,
> Leaving Earth all behind,
> And are borne to the hall,
> Where the soul is refined
> From the grossness of Earth, and made free as the
> mind."

I think my reader will allow that the foregoing is verse of no mean order. An American journal, misled, on the first appearance of "A Lyric of the Morning Land," into supposing the poem to be written by a Mr. Leavitt, passed on it the following comments: "From the reading of Mr. Leavitt's 'Lyric of the Morning Land,' the mind reverts so much to 'Queen Mab,' that one cannot help thinking the poetic mantle of Shelley hath truly fallen upon Mr. Leavitt's shoulders." I need not adopt this extremely eulogistic view; but neither must we permit ourselves to imitate the critic who penned it, who, when he discovered that the poem in question was by Mr. Harris, and professed to be composed under spiritual influence, treated it very differently. Nevertheless, one feels that one labours, in this matter, under the likelihood of a twofold difficulty. One's first tendency, on hearing that a poem claims to proceed from such a source, is to expect that it will be great rubbish; and the result may be that when, to our surprise, we find it not to be rubbish, we then imagine it to be better than it really is. It is equally possible, however, that warned by this well-known tendency, we may be unwilling to acknowledge its real merits, and so finally detract from them. Be this as it may, I can but express my own opinion with cautious moderation, and by copious extracts enable the reader to judge for himself whether I have been too moderate, or not moderate enough. Surely the following passage is strikingly lyrical :—

> " Why is the red rose sweet ?
>   Say, canst thou tell ?
> Say, how do glad hearts beat
>   In earthly shell ?
> No outward wisdom knows,
>   No tongue can tell :
>   No—no—no.
>
> " Hearts with love that glow,
> Roses while they blow,
>   Each in twilight dell
>   Hid away
>   From the day,
>   Neither may
> Disclose the spell.

> " Since thou canst not find
>   How the rose-tree blows,
>   Or what loves combined
>   Form the living rose,
>   Why, oh why,
>   Vainly try
>   To espy
>   How unfold
>   Flowers of gold in poet's breast ;
>   By what art are drest,
>   Angel-thoughts in words of time,
>   Angel-songs in outward rhyme ?"

Besides the poetical distinction these lines may fairly claim, they convey a fresh and further account of the *modus operandi* by which they and all their fellows come to be born. The following stanzas, too, deserve to be reproduced for similar reasons :—

> " Body and Soul are interwed,
>   As light and fire in mingled splendour ;
>   And where the Inner Soul doth tread,
>   The obedient forms delight to tend her.

> " We change to Angels by degrees ;
>   We rise to heaven, but not by dying ;
>   We cross no dark tumultuous seas ;
>   We leave no form in graveyard lying.

> " We change, unfolding, through our love,
>   An inner form of purer essence,
>   Until we rise to heaven above,
>   And worship in the Father's presence."

The religious tone is maintained throughout; and in many places we are reminded of Dr. Newman's "Dream of Gerontius." Do not the ensuing verses read like the wail of the disembodied spirit in that poem ?—

> "Oh! life of love in heaven,
>   For thee I yearn;
>   Yet, from bright morn to even,
>   I turn—I turn.
>
> "The heavens are all receding;
>   Once more I tread,
>   With feet all bruised and bleeding,
>   Earth's regions dead.
>
> "Tumult and storm roll terribly beneath me,
>   And mortal Night
>   Seeks with its woes and agonies to wreath me—
>   But still there's light."

It must not be supposed, however, that "A Lyric of the Morning Land" contains nothing of a more secular and lighter character, as the following commencement of "The Song of the Violet" will show :—

> "There came a fairy blue, and sang:
>   'O maiden dear, attend—attend!
> When first on earth the violet sprang,
>   Each earthly maid had fairy friend.

" ' Who whispered in her ear by night—
    Sing, Heart, my heart, the mellow lay—
And so the violet grew more bright
    Within her eyes from day to day.'

" Wake, fairies, wake, from field and glen—
    Wake, fairies, on your azure steep;
For ye shall throng to earth again,
    And sing to maidens in their sleep."

As a specimen of Mr. Harris's power of poetical narration, I will quote just a few lines from " The Marriage of Apollo," in the same poem :—

" There dwelt in Saturn's ancient reign
    A kingly maiden largely blest;
    There came from regions in the west
A lordly youth her heart to gain—
Chant manfully this manly strain—
He bore aloft Apollo's lyre;
In his full breast he bred a choir
Of azure-crested doves, that fed
On marriage-blossoms; round his head
A changeful sun-crown shone and shone,
And round his snow-white shape was thrown,
A wingèd scarf all gold and blue;
This robe his kingly form shone through;
The lifeblood chorused from his veins,
And, where he trod, the flowery plains
Drank purple radiance from his feet.

     *   *   *   *   *

> His shoulder bore a golden bow;
> White arrows, pure as virgin snow,
> Barbëd with fires, were placed within
> A quiver formed of moonbeams thin,
> Changed into crystals. Whence he came
> None knew; but horses winged with flame
> Appeared above an amber cloud."

I have done my best to arrive at a dispassionate opinion; yet I cannot hesitate to say, that from this last passage, Mr. Leighton might well draw almost literal inspiration for another of his classical pictures; and that if all the passages quoted had been composed by any poet living, they would certainly not have detracted from his reputation.

I cannot say that in any other of his poems Mr. Harris falls below the level of "A Lyric of the Morning Land." As it is probable that very few (if any) of my readers are acquainted with them, I feel all the more bound to give them abundant opportunities of judging for themselves of their literary merits. For "Regina: a Song of Many Days," a similar origin is claimed as for the work we have been considering; this being asserted, and the poem being introduced, in the following melodious strain :—

" Where the rose-tree buds unbar,
  Where the purple pansies are,
  Where the crimson wildings play
  With the last-blown mountain may,
  Fairies are all glad and gay.

" Where the snowy owlet sails,
  Where the tender gloom prevails,
  For the crypt of ages old,
  Lyric wine of amber gold
  Flows for thee, O poet bold !

" Holy men of long ago,
  Come, with faces all aglow:
  Underneath the fretted stones
  Pale Tradition sleeps and moans;'
  But above are angel-tones.

" It is the sweetest night that ever fell;
  And as the young bird, that forsakes its shell,
  Thrilled by the ardours of the mother-dove,
  Who bosoms it with unextinguished love,
  A spirit-poem, Earth's delightful guest,
  Leaps to its life of music through my breast."

Not for the purpose of accusing Mr. Tennyson
of plagiarism, but in order to shield Mr. Harris
against the possible accusation of plagiarising
from him, it is only right to add that the above
passage was published before our Poet Laureate

conceived, or at least expressed, his charming idea of the music of the nightingale sleeping in the little eggs of the parent-bird. The mention of parallelism to Mr. Tennyson suggests a much closer one with Mr. Swinburne; for long before that erratic lyrist burst upon our ken, Mr. Harris had written his " Farewell to Summer," which, save for its clear pure atmosphere, might have been struck from the peculiarly melodious chords of the lyre of the author of the " Songs and Ballads :"--

> " The chimes of the lyrical summer,
> 　　The tones of the bird and the bee,
> That tunefully met the newcomer
> 　　With airs of an infantile glee,
> 　　Dissolve on the lips of the sea.

> " What ships of the blessed are sailing,
> 　　In light o'er the hyaline floor,
> Afar in the sunset unveiling,
> 　　Remote from the vapoury shore,
> 　　Soft visions, returning no more !

> " Young children with zephyr-like dances,
> 　　They dimple the musical sands;
> The ocean, with queenly advances,
> 　　Enfolds them with crystalline bands,
> 　　White roses and pearls from her hands.

> " My heart, on the breast of the ocean,
>   Reclines in a tremulous rest;
> It vibrates with musical motion,
>   It chimes to the songs of the blest;
>   It sings of the summer possest.
>
> " Here all things that greet me are emblems
>   Of life, in the newness begun;
> Yon ocean a radiant semblance,
>   That rolls to the smile of the sun,
>   Of peace that by loving is won.
>
> " Roll on, in thy beautiful being,
>   Glad ocean, with music afar;
> Life bears me to meet the Allseeing,
>   Where all the beatified are,
>   With space at my feet like a star."

This piece was composed in 1859, and published in 1860; and it is a wonderful anticipation of the style, manner, and music of Mr. Swinburne. Indeed, it is just such a poem as Mr. Swinburne might produce in a moment of special inspiration. So far, however, he has, in my opinion, produced nothing so perfect and gem-like. One quotation more, and I will pass from " Regina" :—

> " Pausing by this delicious shore,
> I chant the songs that bubble o'er
>   From some diviner sea,
>   That ebbless flows in me.

> " Whence do the poets' thoughts descend,
> To words of wingèd flame, that tend,
>   Or drop, in vocal rain,
>   Upon the thirsty plain?

> " We are but instruments, that thrill
> Responsive to His lyric will,
>   Who pours the seas, like sand,
>   In sunshine from His hand."

Mr. Harris's longest and most ambitious poem has yet to be mentioned. This is "A Lyric of the Golden Age;" and its birth is distinctly prophesied in the closing lines of "A Lyric of the Morning Land":

> " Another lyric sleeps within
> Thy bosom now.   .   .   .
> Ere hath fallen winter's snow,
> Love shall sing, love shall wake,
> Poets' hearts an Eden make."

It was early on Friday morning, October 19, while Mr. Brittan—of whom I shall have more to say presently—was conversing with Mr. Harris, that the latter was suddenly entranced, and commenced telling him straight off, in prose, the objects the spirits designed to accomplish. The account is too long for me to transcribe; but it may be found at page 23 of the Introduction to the work of which I am treating. Neither can I attempt to give an analysis of the poem. Again, I must be content with extracts. They shall be but two in number, and as unlike as possible to any yet quoted. Here is the first. A spectral column is chanting through the midnight gloom:—

> " Yes, the aged world is dead—
>   Dead are all its mystic dreams;
> Angels from its thought are fled,
>   Angels from its groves and streams !
>   Faith is lost, and being fled,
>   In its loss the world is dead.
>
> " Yes, the aged world is dead—
>   Mirth is gone from court and shrine;
> And a sensual pall is spread
>   O'er the tomb of life divine.
>   Hope is lost, and being fled,
>   In its loss the world is dead.
>
> " Yes, the aged world is dead—
>   Cold the heart, and dim the brain;
> Wise men filch the orphan's bread,
>   Fate and hate in temples reign.
>   Love is lost, and being fled,
>   In its loss the world is dead.
>
> " Then through all the midnight speeding,
>   Like the wind Euroclydon
> O'er the sounding seas receding,
>   Swept the stormy chorus on.

> The day of burning comes at last,
>   The world is dead—the world is dead!
> Spring, summer, autumn, winter past—
>   Youth, manhood, age, like vapours fled.
>   Alas! Alas!
>
> " Sun, moon, and stars—groves, fields, and flowers;
>   Ye pass away, ye pass away!
> Shrines, temples, minarets, and towers,
>   Ye are but tombs where minds decay.
>   Alas! Alas!"

This is indeed a noble wail; and though it lacks the dash of cultivated doubt, the " pathetic minor," characteristic of Mr. Matthew Arnold's lyre, it recalls analogous lines of his, quoted on another occasion. I have been much perplexed to decide what should be the third and last quotation from this strange poem, abounding as it does in remarkable passages. I have, however, fixed on one (much curtailed), in which Mr. Harris, or rather the spirits speaking through him, described the necessary attributes of the poet :—

> " He should be universal as the light :
>   He should have power to draw from common things
>   Essential truth, and, rising o'er all fear
>   Of papal devils and of pagan gods,
>   Should recognize all spirits as his friends,

And see the worst but harps of golden string
Discordant now, but destined at the last
To thrill, inspired with God's own harmony,
And make sweet music with the heavenly host.
He should be wise in simple things, and take
Delight in childhood, and to every child
Be near as Nature, fragrant as the rose ;
Suggesting by his presence and his smile
A world above the natural. . . . .
He should be sceptical of all things base,
And charitable of the faults of men,
Discriminating 'twixt the faults that come
From the young heart, undisciplined, unwise,
But over-brimmed with generous impulses,
Even as a crystal cup too full of wine,
And those lean vices bred in monkish souls
That neither multiply immortal deeds
By marriage of eternal Truth and Love
In their own natures, nor behold the deeds
Of other men, bold, free, and beautiful,
Without attainting them as traitors all.
                He should hold
His gift in reverence.   He should mould his life
In Beauty's perfect fashion, holding on,
Columbus-like, through floods of thought unknown,
Till tropic archipelagos of song,
Till virgin continents of stately verse,
Repay the bold adventure.   Not elate
By sudden joy, like maudlin fools with wine,
He should remain the lord of his new realms,
A godlike sovereign, ruling his sweet verse,
Like Prospero in his enchanted isle.
He should partake the bounty of the world,

> As if he were the universal guest.
> Death should grow beautiful at his approach,
> And doff its starless mantle of the night,
> And stand apparelled in empurpled gold,
> And open that wide wonder-world that lies
> Beyond the confines of mortality;
> And radiant Genii, ruling each a world
> Of choiring Cherubim, should be his friends."

I fancy there will be no two opinions about the lofty poetical eloquence of this passage, which is of course finer still in its complete state. But, when that is granted, how about the spiritualistic origin claimed for it? That, I dare-say, will interest many of my readers far more than its literary features. To this point, then, let me betake myself. I have mentioned the name of Mr. S. B. Brittan, of New York. He is, in a sense, the editor of Mr. Harris's poems. He has constantly acted as amanuensis to Mr. Harris, whilst the latter, played on by the spirits, was delivering himself of his verse; and he it is who has written a long preface to the poem we have last been considering. In it he informs us that the first half of "A Lyric of the Golden Age" was dictated at the Irving House, in New York, at intervals in the course of December and January, 1854-5. During the progress of the delivery, a number of ladies and gentlemen were present from time to time, for the purpose of observing the results of spiritual agency as developed through him. Of these he names Professor Mapes, Dr. and Mrs. Warner, a Mr. Evangelidis from Athens, Mr. Green (an artist), Mr. and Mrs. Burroughs, of the Irving House, Mrs. Dow, Messrs. Partridge, Fishbough, and himself. The persons mentioned are, naturally enough, unknown to me, but there, at any rate, are their names. I wish I could transcribe the whole of what Mr. Brittan calls the " mundane history of the poem," in which he gives the most minute account of what happened on the various occasions of its delivery, which occupied altogether about ninety-four hours — "the greater part being dictated with a rapidity only limited by the capacity of the amanuensis to follow the utterance." I ought to add that Mr. Brittan, though the principal, was not the only amanuensis ; and that during the greater portion of the time thus employed, Mr. Harris's sensation was either wholly suspended, or greatly diminished, and he seemed to be quite oblivious of external circumstances and objects.

And who, it may be asked, is Mr. Lake

Harris, who thus professes to communicate to us
the productions of the poetical spirits of the
other world, and who, in any case, can certainly
produce some very remarkable poetry of his
own? Mr. Harris is an Englishman—I believe
a Yorkshireman—by birth; but he accompanied
his parents to America, in 1827, when he was
only three years old; consequently, he is now
forty-six years of age. He was for a long time
a noted preacher of the Universalist denomina-
tion of New York. He subsequently visited
his native land: the exquisite poem I have
quoted, "Farewell to Summer," having been
composed, I believe, at Whitby, from which
place he dates several other sets of verses,
written in 1859—none of these, however, as far
as I can make out, claiming any supernatural
origin. I do not know how long Mr. Harris
remained in this country; but about 1863 I find
him back in the United States, at Amenia,
Duchess county, prospering as a banker and
agriculturist. In October, 1867, however, he had
a direct intimation from God's Spirit, in obedience
to which he founded, in Chatauqua county, on the
southerly shore of Lake Erie, a community,
whose principle, or "pivot," is "Open or Divine

Respiration." Eight hundred acres were bought by Mr. Harris himself, and as many more have been purchased with the money of the associates, the whole being held by him in trust for the community. Its adult members number about sixty. There is also a hired corps of labourers, mostly Swedes, who are employed because the members themselves, though all working diligently, are not sufficient for the purpose. I do not profess at all to understand what "Open or Divine Respiration" is, though I have given it my best attention; but when I have said that Swedenborg furnishes the doctrinal and philosophical bases of the fabric, to which Mr. Harris has been led by Providence to add other and vital matters, and that the views of the community on love and marriage are severely orthodox, with certain supersensual notions superadded, the germs at least of which may be found in that strange work, Swedenborg's "Conjugial Love," I shall have done accurate justice to Mr. Harris's scheme. One more remarkable fact in connection with it remains to be mentioned. One of Mr. Harris's companions at Chatauqua is no less a personage than Mr. Laurence Oliphant, the author of "The Russian Shores of the Black

Sea," "Minnesota, or the Far West," etc., who was the private secretary of Lord Elgin, when that nobleman was (in 1857) sent as Minister Plenipotentiary to China, then for a time the English representative in Japan, and afterwards for a brief period, M.P. for the Stirling Burghs. He was once a person of considerable note among us; and he now, we are told, "finds his harmonious destiny in digging in the soil on the shore of Lake Erie, in the name of the Lord." With him is his mother, Lady Oliphant; and with her, her former lady's-maid, " living together on terms of perfect equality."

I shall revert to Mr. Harris and his poems before I close this chapter; but here it becomes necessary to state, that he by no means stands alone in his claims to be a mere harp in the hands of invisible spirits. I am, however, acquainted with only one other individual advancing such pretensions, whose poetry excites curiosity by virtue of its goodness. This is Miss Lizzie Doten, whose "Poems from the Inner Life" now lie before me. In a simply and sensibly-written preface, she states her experiences from childhood upwards. The volume is divided into two portions. The first or smaller portion contains compositions, avowedly "wrought out of the brain by the slow process of thought;" the second and larger one consists of communications under spirit-influence. The names of particular spirits communicating were not discernible by her in every instance. As a rule, however, they were; and among them figure the names of Edgar Allan Poe, Burns, and Shakespeare. The communications of the first were the most frequent; and I must be content with quoting part of one poem professing to come from that source. It may add to the interest with which many people will read it, if I state that Mr. Anthony Trollope was present at its delivery in America, and was much struck by the scene and the poem. Its name is "The Kingdom":

> " 'Twas the ominous month of October—
> How the memories rise in my soul!
> How they swell like a sea in my soul!
> When a spirit, sad, silent, and sober,
> Whose glance was a word of control,
> Drew me down to the dark Lake Avernus,
> In the desolate kingdom of Death—
> To the mist-covered Lake of Avernus,
> In the ghoul-haunted kingdom of Death.

> " And there, as I shivered and waited,
> I talked with the souls of the dead—

> With those whom the living call dead;
> The lawless, the lone, and the hated,
> Who broke from their bondage and fled—
> From madness and misery fled.
> Each word was a burning eruption,
> That leapt from a crater of flame—
> A red lava-tide of corruption,
> That out of life's sediment came,
> From the scoriac nature God gave them,
> Compounded of glory and shame.
>
> "It was there the Eumenides found us,
> In sight of no shelter or shore—
> No beacon or light from the shore:
> They lashed up the white waves around us,
> We sank in the waters' wild roar;
> But not to the regions infernal,
> Through billows of sulphurous flame,
> But unto the City Eternal,
> The Home of the Blessed, we came."

Arriving at the gate of the Beautiful City, one of the company, "a proud prelate," addresses—

> "A beautiful, beautiful child,
> A golden-haired, azure-eyed child,"

who is standing "in the midst of the mystical splendour," and claims to be admitted to heaven by virtue of his sins having been forgiven, and his soul washed clean by the orthodox method :—

"The child stood in silence and wonder,
  Then bowed down her beautiful head;
  And even as fragrance is shed
From the lilacs the waves have swept under,
  She meekly and tenderly said,
  So simply and truthfully said:
'In vain do ye seek to behold Him;
  He dwells in no temple apart;
The height of the heavens cannot hold Him,
  And yet He is here in my heart—
  He is here, and He will not depart.'

"Then out from the mystical splendour,
  The swift-changing, crystalline light,
  The rainbow-hued, scintillant light,
Gleamed faces more touching and tender
  Than ever had greeted our sight—
  Our sun-blinded, death-darkened sight;
And they sang: 'Welcome home to the kingdom,
  Ye earth-born and serpent-beguiled!
The Lord is the light of this kingdom,
  And His temple the heart of a child—
  Of a trustful and teachable child;
Ye are born to the life of the kingdom—
  Receive and believe as a child.'"

It will probably be confessed, on all hands,
that this is a very beautiful little poem, and—if
in nothing else, at any rate in style—an admirable imitation of Edgar Allan Poe. But it is an
imitation, and nothing more, some will say.
Possibly; in my opinion, probably, if not cer-

tainly. Miss Lizzie Doten, however, asseverates that it is nothing of the kind. " The first poem," she says in her preface, " delivered by Poe came to me far more unexpectedly than any other. The supposition has been presented, that I, or the one who wrote the poem, must have been very familiar with the writings of Poe. As no one wrote the poem for me, consequently I am the only one that can answer to the supposition ; and I can say, most conscientiously, that previous to that time, I had never read, to my knowledge, any of his poems, save ' The Raven,' and I had not seen that for several years. Indeed, I have read, comparatively speaking, very little poetry in the course of my life, and have never made the style of any author a study. I can describe the influence of Poe as a species of mental in-toxication. After giving one of his poems, I was usually quite ill for several days."

As regards a prior acquaintance by her with the writings of Poe, I can only express the opinion, that Miss Doten is labouring under some mistake ; and though this opinion will probably be shared by most people, without any proof at all, I may as well confirm it by indirect but, to my thinking, very forcible testimony. In

the same preface, Miss Doten says : " Among
the spiritual poems will be found two purporting
to come from Shakespeare. I do not think that
the poems in themselves come up to the productions of his master-mind." They do not—indeed,
they are poor in the extreme.

But before drawing the obvious inference
from this fact, let me, as I promised, revert for
a moment to Mr. Lake Harris. Considerable
portions of " A Lyric of the Golden Age," though
none that I have quoted, purport to come from
Byron, Shelley, Keats, and Pollok; and Mr.
Harris, on other occasions, has been inspired
also by Poe. But mark the result ! His professed messages from Poe are just as excellent,
and as strikingly resemble the known and in-
disputable compositions of that writer, as those
transmitted by him through Miss Doten. What
proceeds from Pollok is very superior to anything that ever proceeded from that very blank
rhymester in his natural condition; what professes to come from Shelley and Keats strongly
recalls the compositions in the flesh of those two
glorious bards, but recalls them only to suggest
a painful absence of their real *afflatus;* whilst
the "Prophecy," attributed to the spirit of

Byron, has absolutely nothing in common with the earthly utterances of that supreme singer but the Spenserian metre of " Childe Harold." Are not the facts obvious, and is not the inference inevitable ? I have no wish to depreciate Poe's poetical faculties ; but his poems are peculiarly imitable, and Mr. Harris and Miss Doten imitate them equally well. Pollok's poetry is not poetry at all, but mere rubbish—sometimes tame, sometimes pompous ; and Mr. Harris, who is a poet, could not possibly write down to it. Of Shelley and Keats, the manner, and even the sentiments, are to be simulated, but the real soul and aroma are beyond imitation ; and this is precisely what happened to Mr. Harris, when inspired by them. But Shakespeare and Byron, the Dioscuri of English song, utterly baffle imitation; and whilst Mr. Harris's communications from the one bear no resemblance to his known productions, the communications from the other, on Miss Doten's own confession, " scarcely come up to that master-mind."

Do I then intend to propound the conclusion, that Mr. Lake Harris and Miss Lizzie Doten are conscious impostors, trying to palm off upon us natural compositions as supernatural compositions? Not at all. To say nothing of the lady, of whose good faith I am amply satisfied, the man who could write, of his own accord, such poetry as I have quoted from Mr. Harris's works, and found so honest, and in many respects admirable, a community as the one I have described, could not well have any inducement to play the part of a literary rogue. I do not say the thing is absolutely impossible, but it is to the last degree improbable. Nor does it seem to me at all necessary to fall back upon so harsh a supposition, in order to question the origin Mr. Harris himself ascribes to his poetry. I believe him to be a victim, partly to his own imagination, and partly to the rapidity with which, no doubt, much of his poetry, so to speak, flows from him. In Mr. Brittan's preface to "An Epic of the Starry Heaven" occurs the following extract from Mozart's own account of the way in which he came by some of his happiest musical compositions :—

"When all goes well with me—when I am in a carriage, or walking, or when I cannot sleep at night—the thoughts come streaming in upon me most fluently; whence, or how, is more than I can tell. Then follow the counterpoint and the clang of the different instruments ; and if I am not disturbed, my soul is fixed, and the thing grows greater, and broader, and clearer ; and I have it all in my head, even when the piece is a long one ; and I see it like a beautiful picture—not hearing the beautiful parts in succession, as they must be played, but the whole at once. That is the delight."

No doubt. And any truly inspired artist, whether poet, painter, or musician, must have had similar experiences. But to such inspirations most people will probably think it quite unnecessary to attach any more definite meaning than has hitherto been involved in that phrase. There is no serious pretence that Mr. Harris or Miss Doten all at once improvised excellent poems, without any premeditation. Miss Doten's account is, that "they were not like lightning flashes, coming unheralded. Several days before they were given, I had intimations of them. Oftentimes I would awake from a deep slumber, and detached fragments would be floating through my mind." Again, in the case of Mr. Harris's "A Lyric of the Morning Land," a period of as long as from January to August elapsed before "the archetypal ideas, internally unwrought, descended into the externals of the mind, uttered themselves in speech, and were transcribed as spoken by the Medium." If we except the strangeness of its phraseology, this account does not much differ from the account many, if not most, poets would give of the genesis of their compositions. Superadd a firm faith in Spiritualism apart from poetry, and the beliefs and states of Mr. Harris, of Miss Doten, and others, become not altogether unintelligible.

I daresay that impartial people will still be of opinion that a residuum of difficulty remains behind, which must be explained either by the imputation of a little touch of imposture, or by granting that there is something more in Spiritualism than is usually allowed. Be this as it may, I have thought it necessary, whilst attempting to take a more or less comprehensive view of the " Poetry of the Period," to give an account of this little-known and obscure branch of it. Its literary merits, I think, are obvious. Not so evident, perhaps, are its faults; but to these I am by no means blind. The poetry I have been reviewing is often more remarkable for sound than sense ; though, generally, the two are fairly combined. It is rather monotonous in tone, deficient in very decided originality, and too suggestive of the works of other poets whose style and manner of thought are most easily copied. There is nothing in it to raise our estimate of the " Poetry of the Period ;" but it must candidly be said that it fully deserves to be mentioned in connection with it, and is worthy of the age which is its real parent, if scarcely of that invisible land to which it ascribes its birth.

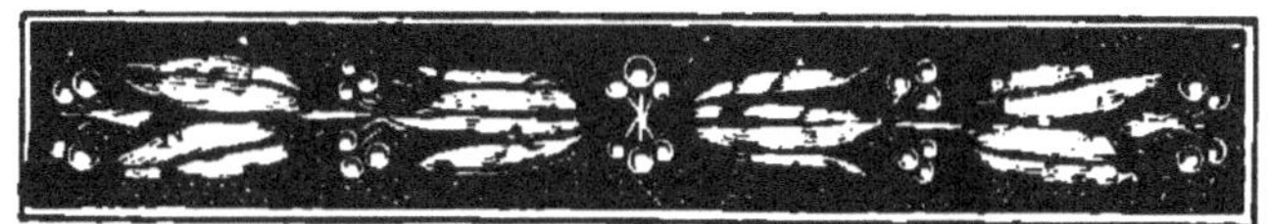

Summary.

THE reader who has been good enough to peruse the critical essays in which I have attempted to appraise the writings of Mr. Tennyson, Mr. Browning, Mr. Swinburne, Mr. Arnold, Mr. Morris, and others, cannot have failed already to perceive that it was not without good reason (or, at any rate, without serious design) that I comprehended the works of them all under the appellation of "The Poetry of the Period." He will have noticed that I have completely overlooked any mere faults of detail with which their verse may be infected—have abstained from all inquiry into what may be called their literary peculiarities and individual intellectual deficiencies — have never for one moment separated them from the age in which they write; but that, whilst refusing to them, one and all, the faintest claim to be regarded as great poets, I have rather intimated my astonishment that, under the circumstances, their productions should be as good as they are. Of course it is possible that I form an exaggerated estimate of their worth, since none of us can help having some sympathy with the productions of the period in which we too "live, move, and have our being," and that posterity, necessarily still more impartial, will think less of them even than I do. It is quite certain, however, it will not think more of them. I desire in this summary to make that important point more definitely clear.

For it is one of the most common but most superficial of errors, and one whose predominance in a scientific age is singularly unpardonable, to suppose that poetry, and indeed all art, is exclusively an affair partly of individual inclination, and partly of public patronage. The notion is radically false in both particulars. As far as individuals with a natural bent for the production of poetry are concerned, it is highly and antecedently probable that the number is pretty constant through successive generations. That it is variable can never by any possibility be proved. On the other hand, what the world can do for a poet in any particular age is just as much beyond its control as his own genius is beyond his—every age having a decided bent, just as absolutely as every individual. Very little reflection suffices to show that, if such be the case, the perseverance of the latter will be of little avail, supposing the disposition of the former to be opposed to it. It is the nature of an apple-tree to grow apples, and to shed its leaves; but take it to Ceylon, it becomes undeciduous, and bears no more fruit. The tree cannot help itself, neither can the people of Ceylon. The conditions under which apples are produced having been removed, naturally enough apples likewise disappear. The person who does not see that his own species—or any variation of it, *e.g.* poets—will equally, though, of course, not quite so obviously, suffer modification by a complete shifting of the conditions, is not much indebted to his epoch for the only thing, save material comfort, it has got to give him particularly worth having—viz., an appreciation of the universality and permanence of law. If he be an ordinarily intelligent person, he can have no difficulty in understanding that the individual, whether poet, painter, statesman, or philosopher, must be largely indebted for what of excellent or defective there is in him, to the age, people, and intellects by which he is surrounded. They are his atmosphere—his soil, sun, sky—in a word, his climate. In speaking of Mr. Tennyson, I remarked that, could we imagine him transplanted to the Elizabethan era, he would have been a much smaller poet than he is now, and probably the mere writer of a few courtly masques; whereas, if we could imagine Shakespeare transplanted into ours, he would very likely not have worked as a poet at all—or, if he had persisted in following his bent, have been considerably inferior, in work done, to the actual Mr. Tennyson with whom we are acquainted. The explanation, of course, is that the climate of the Elizabethan age was so fine and bracing—so favourable, in fact, to the growth and development of one predisposed to be a really great poet—that Mr. Tennyson would have been nipped to the ground, and where he now daintily clambers would have been compelled to crawl; whilst the climate of the Victorian era, on the contrary, is so relaxing, that where Mr. Tennyson thrives and luxuriates to the full extent of his natural capacity, Shakespeare, like the tree transplanted to the equator, would have apparently changed his whole nature, and ceased altogether to bear poetical fruit.

This, then, is the real truth of the matter—that great poetry is, like everything else, an affair indispensably of external conditions, since the existence of the internal conditions may be presumed, and can never be proved to be absent. But the presence or absence of the requisite external conditions is demonstrable, and no one who has formed any approach to a just idea of the essential conditions for the production of great poetry, or great art of any sort, can doubt, not only that they are absent in the present age, but that actively hostile conditions are ruling in their stead. What publishers call a " demand" for poetry on the part of the reading public, and what severe critics would call an itch for versifying on the part of innumerable gentlemen and ladies, have nothing on earth to do with the production of great or even fairly good poetry. The versifying mania has raged in all known epochs with about equal severity—thus fortifying the presumption that mere individual proclivities are pretty constant generation after generation—

and certainly there is no abatement of the disease just at present. The words of Garin d'Apchier are just as applicable now as they were in the days of the Troubadours: "Les jougleurs se sont multipliés au point qu'il y en a autant que de lapins dans une garenne : on en est inondé." How little their quantity contributes to improve their quality, let any impartial person decide. Just as little is its quality affected by the "demand" for it, which during the last five or six years, at any rate, has been very remarkable. For art is not like dry-goods, whatever some people may think or indolently assume to the contrary. The law of demand and supply breaks down when once you pass the limits of craft, and invade the region of art. Though the material and labour requisite for the production of art must be paid for somehow, all the money in the world cannot produce one stroke of art, any more than it can produce the notes of a nightingale. The proper conditions alone can produce that, and demand is not one of them, much less all of them. Financial patronage—whether it be the patronage of wealthy, cultured dilettanti, of a luxurious, getting-on, and aspiring public, or of a centralized and tasteful State—is equally powerless to evoke manifestations of art if the social conditions are wanting to its development. Financial patronage may found academies, distribute prizes, confer laureateships, instigate unbounded competition. But what then? Great art, whether it be poetry or any other of its branches, bears as much resemblance to birthday odes, or poems that run through innumerable editions, as a monarch of the forest does to a faultless park-paling, or a wind-stirred group of water-reeds to an exquisitely-finished cane-bottomed chair. Naturally this age, having plenty of money, and having procured with it an immense amount of desirable things—underground railways, ocean steamers, splendid carriages and horses, rare and long-kept vintages, enormous mirrors, miles of lace, new colours, exciting novels by eminent hands, newspapers without end, gorgeous spectacles, naked dancing-girls, deft cooks, many courses, and a mild religion—is desirous of having great art likewise, which it has always heard is a good thing, and which, moreover, it fancies that it has got. For why should it not have it? It is quite ready to pay for it. To pay what for it? That is the question. Ready money. Alas! ready money is not

the price of great art. Great art is to be reached
only through spontaneity, simplicity, faith, unconscious earnestness, and manly concentration.
It is idle to inquire if the age would make a
sacrifice of its artificiality, its self-consciousness,
its feminine infirmities, its scepticism, its distracted aims, in order to obtain it, since it would
argue a complete metamorphosis of the age into
something different from what it is ; and ages
are just as powerless to change their character
as leopards to change their skins. It can offer
money, favourable criticisms, and the *entrée* to
its most conspicuous drawing-rooms—for it has
got these things to give. But the contemporary
social atmosphere and climate are no more within
its gift or control than is the direction of the
winds, the stir of volcanoes, the tumult of the
sea, or the electricity of the air. These are not
the commodities of market overt, and the heavens
have not yet been assailed by the law of demand
and supply.

Here, then, we touch firm ground. We bring
the poet *en rapport* with his age, and at best he
can but say what he has got to say. The more
his own disposition is in harmony with that of
his time, the more complete, lucid, and satis-

factory will be his poetry. If he clashes with it, the conflict will be evident in his verse—with discord, incompleteness, and obscurity as the result. It stands to reason that it must be so ; for the resultant of two forces pushing in much the same direction is of necessity both simpler and stronger than that of the two forces pulling in different directions. Of this truth Mr. Tennyson is a most remarkable example. He has never once, as I have previously remarked, betrayed the slightest symptom of possessing the highest of poetical gifts. There is not one sublime passage in the whole of his works ; and, what is more, there is no attempt at one. Yet I repeat my opinion that he must be conceded the first place among living English poets, though some of them have occasionally aimed at higher flights than any he has dreamed of. For whilst they are partly of the age, and partly at issue with it, he is of his age almost wholly and solely. Take, for instance, his idea of the poet; it will illustrate my meaning excellently well, particularly when we compare it with that entertained by poets of a very different calibre.

> " The poet in a golden clime was born,
>   With golden stars above,"

Mr. Tennyson tells us; and he goes on to speak of his thoughts—

> "Filling with light

> "And vagrant melodies the winds which bore
>   Them earthward till they lit;
>   Then, like the arrow-seeds of the field-flower,
>   The fruitful wit,

> "Cleaving, took root, and springing forth anew
>   Where'er they fell, behold,
>   Like to the mother-plant in semblance, grew
>   A flower all gold.

> "Thus truth was multiplied on truth, the world
>   Like one great garden showed,
>   And through the wreaths of floating dark upcurled,
>   Rare sunrise flowed."

The poem, no doubt, is well known to my readers; and they will remember how Freedom is next invoked, with "no blood upon her maiden robes," and then Wisdom, of whom it is said that she was armed with only one poor poet's scroll, and that

> ". . . . . No sword
>   Of wrath her right arm whirled."

I have not quoted this as a specimen of Mr. Tennyson's best manner—for, verily, it is rather artificial stuff—but as showing the tone of his

mind on a cardinal point with which his own
vocation and genius are indissolubly associated.
In another short poem on the same subject, the
view taken of the poet's ground and function
is equally characteristic, and, if anything, still
smaller :—

> " Vex not thou the poet's mind.
>
> .   .   .   .   .   .
>
> Clear and bright it should be ever,
> Flowing like a crystal river."

The ground wherein he dwells is not to be
invaded by the " dark-brow'd sophist."   Everything therein is holy water, spicy flowers,
and laurel-shrubs; and it is thus finally described :—

> " In the heart of the garden the merry bird chants.
>
> .   .   .   .
>
> In the middle leaps a fountain,
>   Like sheet lightning
>   Ever brightening
> With a low melodious thunder;
> All day and all night it is ever drawn
>   From the brain of the purple mountain,
>   Which stands in the distance yonder :
> It springs on a level of flowery lawn,
> And the mountain draws it from Heaven above,
> And it sings a song of undying love."

Did I exaggerate when I said that Mr.
Tennyson is the tenant of the garden? To
be such is evidently his own *beau ideal.* To
sing among laurel-shrubs, spicy flowers, sparkling
fountains, flowery lawns—behold, according to
his own confession, the "holy ground" of the
poet! There is a mountain in the distance
yonder, but he does not go to it. Mountains
are not for small birds. Hark to a different
strain !—

> "The sky is changed! and such a change! Oh night,
> And storm, and darkness, ye are wondrous strong,
> Yet lovely in your strength, as is the light
> Of a dark eye in woman! Far along
> From peak to peak, the rattling crags among,
> Leaps the live thunder. Not from one lone cloud,
> But every mountain now hath found a tongue,
> And Jura answers through her misty shroud,
> Back to the joyous Alps, who call to her aloud!

> " And this is in the night! Most glorious night!
> Thou wert not sent for slumber! Let me be
> A sharer in thy fierce and far delight,—
> A portion of the tempest, and of thee !
> How the lit lake shines, a phosphoric sea,
> And the big rain comes dancing to the earth !
> And now again 'tis black,—and now the glee
> Of the loud hills shakes with its mountain mirth,
> As though they did rejoice o'er a young earthquake's
> birth.

" Sky, mountains, river, winds, lake, lightnings—ye,
  With night, and clouds, and thunder, and a soul
  To make these felt and feeling, well may be
  Things that have made me watchful; the far roll
  Of your departing voices is the knoll
  Of what in me is sleepless,—if I rest.
  But where of ye, O tempests, is the goal ?
  Are ye like those within the human breast ?
  Or do ye find at length, like eagles, some high nest?

" Could I unbody and unbosom now
  That what is most within me,—could I wreak
  My thoughts upon expression, and thus throw
  Soul, heart, mind, passion, feelings, strong or weak,
  All that I would have sought, and all I seek,
  Own, know, feel, and yet breathe, into *one* word,
  And that one word were lightning, I would speak ;
  But as it is, I live and die unheard,
  With a most voiceless thought, sheathing it as a
    sword."

That is not the Poetry of the Period. Not much
holy water and laurel-shrubs there. It is not a
matter of a purple mountain in the distance, but
of black rattling crags, and the poet is a portion
of them and their tumultuous glee. The mountains have found a tongue, and so has the
poet, but yet not one that contents him. Mr.
Tennyson,

    " Flowing like a crystal river,
      Bright as light, and clear as wind,"

says without difficulty or deficiency what he has got to say; and no wonder. But the greater voice, when it has said immeasurably more, still feels that it has not said a millionth part enough. It will live and die unheard. The one feels that he ought to be hemmed "in the heart of a garden," and accordingly is so. The other yearns "to mingle with the universe," and cannot, altogether. The one is satisfied with a "fountain, like sheet lightning, ever brightening." The other is drawn instinctively to the surging, seductive, but for ever unsurrendering sea :—

> "And I have loved thee, Ocean! and my joy
> Of youthful sports was on thy breast to be
> Borne, like thy bubbles, onward. From a boy
> I wantoned with thy breakers; they to me
> Were a delight; and if the freshening sea
> Made them a terror, 'twas a pleasing fear;
> For I was, as it were, a child of thee,
> And trusted to thy billows far and near,
> And laid my head upon thy mane—as I do here!"

Nothing could more forcibly illustrate the abyss that lies between poetry that is beautiful, and poetry that is great, and between the periods which give birth to each respectively. The present age is set upon being proper, pious, peaceful, complete and respectable. Not that it is necessarily any of the five; but they constitute its ideal. It thinks fighting highly undesirable, if not actually wrong. It hates rows. It regards a loudly avowed disbelief and discontent as disreputable, if not something worse. In reality it entertains doubts about everything, but it is a comfort-loving coward, and takes refuge in a more or less silent compromise. Fancy a poet saying nowadays, as Wordsworth said,

> " Carnage is God's eldest daughter ! "

On the contrary, there is now "no blood upon the maiden robes" of Freedom. Not that, as a fact, there is not plenty of it; we are compelled to fight every now and then, but we do not like it, and we have not manliness enough to exult in it, when nothing but fighting is left. Even when we do fight, we openly profess to fight for our interests, not for right; sighing all the while for the return of peace, laurel-shrubs, fountains, and holy water.

All this, as I have said, proves the feminine, timorous, narrow, domesticated temper of the times, and explains the feminine, narrow, domesticated, timorous Poetry of the Period. Take yet another sign, though it is only a fresh illustration of the same truth—a looking at the old fact in a new light. What is one of the chief marks of great poetry? Surely, action. Indeed, we may say of great poetry, what Demosthenes said of great oratory, that the soul of it is—action, action, action. The "Iliad" is all action. So, almost all, is the "Æneid." Look at the action in "Paradise Lost!" To name the poetry of Shakespeare is to name the poetry of action. What are the "Lady of the Lake," "Marmion," and "Rokeby," but action—action? Byron's early tales bristle with movement; and in "Childe Harold," the inanimate themselves, battlefields, ruins, mountains, sepulchres, the very air, are made to stir with vigorous and active pulses. Turn to Mr. Tennyson, and what do we see? Still life—almost uniform still life. There is motion of a kind—but of what kind? You have the rustling of silks, the blowing of zephyrs, the caracoling of palfreys, the humming of bees, the sighs of lovers; you see leagues of grass washed by slow broad streams, languid pulses of the oar, Orion sloping slowly to the west, stately ships on placid waters, summers crisp with shining woods, all imbedded in exquisite verse, of which it may almost be said, as of the author's own "Sleeping Beauty," that

> "It sleeps, nor dreams, but ever dwells
>   A perfect form in perfect rest."

It wants shaking; but you would shake it in vain. Sound and fury, not always signifying nothing, would not come of it, for they are not there. Mr. Tennyson can speak glibly and well of

> ". . . . greaves and cuisses dash'd with drops
>   By onset;"

but he cannot take us into the onset, and show us how the drops come there, and all the glorious bloody thick of the fight. He can

> ". . . . . take Excalibur
>   And fling him far into the middle mere;"

but he cannot take him into the reek of battle, and make him strike and act. What could possibly be tamer than such lines as the following?—

> "Then Enid waited pale and sorrowful,
>   And down upon him bore the bandit three.
>   And at the midmost charging, Prince Geraint
>   Drave the long spear a cubit through his breast,
>   And out beyond; and then against his brace

> Of comrades, each of whom had broken on him
> A lance that splintered like an icicle,
> Swung from his brand a windy buffet out,
> Once, twice, to right, to left, and stunned the twain,
> Or slew them."

What could be poorer, again, than the description of wild Limours dashing against Geraint?—

> " . . . . . . Who closed with him, and bore
> Down by the length of lance and arm beyond
> The crupper, and so left him stunned or dead,
> And overthrew the next that followed him,
> And blindly rushed on all the rout behind."

In plain English, all that is very miserable, and utterly unworthy of Mr. Tennyson's powers, when exercised on a congenial subject. Many a schoolboy would have described it better. We feel, as we read either of these passages, that the man's heart was not in them. The description is accurate enough, and, in a sense, pictorial; but it smells ineffably of the studio and the lamp. There is no dust, and clang, and hot blood in it. In a word, it too is still life, where still life ought not to be; and nothing can be more certain than that whenever Mr. Tennyson's admirers wish to cite examples of his real poetical powers—and the examples are endless—they will infallibly have to cite passages avowedly to still life belonging. It is surely needless to point out how an instinctive taste and preference for still life is not a masculine, but a feminine propensity ; and equally so, that we have thus a fresh corroboration of the particular charge I have so strongly pressed both against the age and its worthy Laureate.

But there is yet another, though again a kindred, mark by which we may recognize that the Poetry of the Period is not great. No poet of the first rank can be named who has been satisfied with things " of the earth, earthy," as the subject and mechanism of his verse. Homer invades the halls of the celestial gods, Virgil the gloomy abode of the infernals. Milton soars up to Heaven and swoops down to hell, and Dante had already joined to those conquests the purgatory of his more Catholic creed. Shakespeare has his delicate Puck, and his dainty Ariel—

> " To run upon the sharp wind of the north,
> To do me.business in the veins of the earth,
> When it is baked with frost."

Listening to that hyperterrestrial singing, we are forced to exclaim, with Ferdinand :

> " Where should this music be ? i' the air or the earth ?
>   It sounds no more : and, sure, it waits upon
>   Some god o' the island. . . . .
>   . . . . But 'tis gone.
>   No, it begins again. . . . .
>   This is no mortal business, nor no scund
>   That the earth owes. I hear it now above me."

No mortal business, either, is it that we hear
in that magnificent drama bequeathed us by
Byron, in which scandalous imaginations have
recently been groping for corroboration of a
filthy and venal fable. It is at the bidding of
a god of the island, too, that

> " The spirits of the unbounded universe,
>   They who do compass earth about, and dwell
>   In subtler essence—they to whom the tops
>   Of mountains inaccessible are haunts,
>   And earth's and ocean's caves familiar things "—

are compelled, at the will of Manfred, to rise and
appear ! Well might the witch reply :—

> " . . . . Son of Earth !
>   I know thee, and the powers that give thee power : "

when, flinging water into the air, he muttered the
adjuration to the .

> " Beautiful spirit with the hair of light
>   And dazzling eyes of glory, in whose form
>   The charms of earth's least mortal daughters grow
>   To an unearthly stature, in an essence
>   Of purer elements,"

and forced her to commune with him. " The powers which give thee power "—there's the rub ! They gave it to Homer, to Dante, to Milton, to Shakespeare, to Shelley, to Byron, to Goethe. They withhold it—does it not sound almost ludicrous to write the name ?—from Mr. Tennyson. He is of the earth, earthy—very beautiful earth, the very finest possible clay, but clay and, alas ! not spirit. Not to him, nor to any fallen on evil days like ours, has been granted that consummate power, that culminating spell of all, which

> " . . . . bodies forth
>   The forms of things unknown ;
>   Turns them to shape, and gives to airy nothing
>   A local habitation and a name.
>   Such tricks hath strong imagination,"

but strong imagination only. Mr. Tennyson and his contemporaries are often lovely, but never " lovely in their strength." That is a combination wholly beyond them. Mr. Browning, as we have seen, would fain be strong, but is only grotesque, and has unguardedly left us the secret of his process in the closing lines of Sórdello :—

> " .   .   . Spirits are conjectured fair or foul,
>   Evil or good, judicious authors think,
>   According as they vanish in a stink,
>   Or in a perfume. Friends, be frank ; ye snuff
>   Civet, I warrant. Really ? Like enough !
>   Merely the savour's rareness ; any nose
>   May ravish with impunity a rose :
>   Rifle a musk-pod, and 'twill ache like yours !
>   I'd tell you that same pungency ensures
>   An after-gust—but that were overbold.
>   Who would have heard Sordello's story told."

Mr. Browning is both overbold and exceedingly indiscreet, to boot. He has succeeded in securing the attention of a curious and novelty-loving age by the prepense pungency of his ungainly verses ; but he may rest assured, the " after-gust " will be very brief. Literary oddity and acrobatism will not be mistaken by posterity for strength.

But perhaps the most forcible explanation of the fact that the Poetry of the Period, with all its excellent intentions, falls so lamentably short of greatness, remains to be mentioned ; and with it I may fitly bring the subject to a close. So little have art, its nature and necessary conditions, been considered by those who, both in writing

and conversation, make these things their perpetual theme, that they actually point to the
extreme diversity of what they call the art-pro-
ductions of this age, and to the divergence, both
in subject and in treatment, of the various authors
I have mentioned, as a proof of its vast intrinsic
art-producing capacity. Had they the faintest
glimmer of the real truth, they would be aware
that such a fact, if established, is conclusive, in
the event of any difference of opinion on the
subject, against their position. Great poets are
the unambiguous representative voice of decisive
eras that have arrived at some definite conclusion.
Mr. Matthew Arnold, who is honourably distinguished from our unreflecting crowd of critics by
the sobriety of his understanding and the subtle
delicacy of his judgment—and whose opinions,
despite his manifest talents and accomplishments
(which they cannot well challenge), they accordingly hold in but indifferent esteem—has
intimated what an important difference there
is between literature that is "adequate" and
literature that is inadequate. An adequate
literature he finds in the age of Pericles. He
might have added that it is to be found likewise
in the age of Elizabeth, and in the first two

decades of the present century, and that it is lamentably absent in the age of Victoria. As Mr. Arnold has apologised for the incompleteness of the lecture in which he propounds this view, I need not dwell upon the defect he has himself confessed; I can only regret it, and hope that at some future time he will more fully develope a most pregnant observation. Happily, I can introduce what I wish to say under cover of a writer more profound and suggestive even, though unhappily more hasty, than the late occupant of the Poetry chair at Oxford. It is Auguste Comte, who makes the further remark —incidentally indeed, as so many of his most precious remarks are made—that art, in its highest and most satisfactory form, cannot possibly be expected from an epoch and a people whose best and most vivid intellects are not substantially agreed. The truth of the observation will be acknowledged by any one who will take the pains to ask himself two questions: firstly, whether the law as stated is antecedently probable; and secondly, whether it is corroborated by our historical experience—or, in other words, whether the epochs and nations most conspicuous for the production of art to which Mr. Matthew Arnold's epithet of " adequate " may properly be applied, have not been conspicuous for intellectual concord ? Of course nations and epochs have over and over again been stolidly or enthusiastically at one (though rarely the latter), not only without developing art of the highest order, but without developing art of any sort. I need, however, scarcely observe that indispensable conditions are something very different from absolute guarantees.

That the conditions laid down by Comte are truly indispensable will be readily seen when I put the matter in a more homely light. We have already seen that the poet, no matter what his individual temperament and tendencies, cannot hope to contend successfully against an age of opposite temperament and tendencies, and that only by the amicable co-operation of the two can great poetry possibly be produced. The reason of this is that the poet, like anybody and everything else, is very much at the mercy of conditions totally independent of himself. Having thus recalled the enormous effect which it has been shown, is producible on the individual, let us now, since we are in a better condition to do so, estimate the effect likely to be wrought in him by great diversity of simultaneous conditions; and surely it is not only comprehensible, but obvious, that though their extreme diversity may develope in him a larger number of qualities, it will not and cannot develope some one quality to the extent the latter would have been developed had the conditions hostile to it been wholly absent, and the conditions eminently friendly been present exclusively, or, at least, greatly predominated. Now, in an age in which men's opinions, wishes, and modes of thought are consentaneous, these conditions, composing the atmosphere, the climate, of which we spoke, are brought to bear upon the individual to be developed—in the case we are considering, the poet—with full, combined, and undisturbed force. He gets the benefit, or as it may happen, the damage of their collectiveness. If they are too strong for him they overwhelm him, as they would have overwhelmed Mr. Tennyson in the age of Elizabeth, or at the beginning of this century. If they are not too strong for him, but he, on the contrary, is strong enough to be buoyed up by them, they bear him on to the grandest work and the furthest immortality, as in the two epochs I have named they carried

Shakespeare and Byron. Of course, had a Shakespeare or a Byron not been there, their force would have been largely thrown away and wasted, since it is the poorest and most meagre philosophy in the world to suppose, with one school of thinkers, that men are always forthcoming for emergencies. But, again, Shakespeare and Byron had been there in vain, if the force to employ them had been wanting, since it is equally preposterous to suppose that man can make emergencies. It is when you have, to use Mr. Matthew Arnold's admirable phraseology, " a significant, a highly-developed, a *culminating* epoch," that you have the chance (again to have resort to his language) of "a comprehensive, a commensurate, an adequate literature." The one is not infallibly ensured by the other; but where you have not got the first, it is dead certain that you will not get the second.

Now, what is the temper of the age in which we live ? Is intellectual concord one of its characteristics ? On the contrary, is not intellectual discord its very mark and note ? It is an age blown about "with every wind of doctrine." It cannot make up its mind on any one single subject, except that to have plenty of money is a good thing; and even on that point it has occasional miserable qualms of conscience, being ever and anon half-disposed to suspect that, after all, hair shirts and serge are better than purple and fine linen. It entertains the most serious doubts as to Christianity save as an historical phenomenon; and though it cannot bring itself really to believe in the old pagan deities, it would like vastly to revivify them. It is by no means sure even as to the existence of God; and if there be one, what He is like completely baffles its power of deciding. Between the doctrine that men have no souls, and that tables and pianos have, it swings in painful and ludicrous oscillation. What is the best form of government; what the desirable state of society; what man's mission—what woman's; who ought to rule and who obey, or whether anybody ought to obey at all; whether marriage be an obsolete institution, or one deserving of rehabilitation; whether troops of nude dancing-girls be an indecent spectacle, or only an agreeably exciting entertainment: on all these, and indeed on every fundamental matter, it is in a hopeless plight of doubt and bewilderment. It consoles itself by asserting that, if it is wanting in decision, it is

remarkable for toleration. It is a tolerant age.
No doubt it is ; though I may observe it would
be rather extraordinary, not to say scandalous,
if, under the circumstances, it were anything
else. Still, toleration is a good thing, however
brought about, and has its merits. But it has
its drawbacks also, and I will name two of them.
A tolerant age never produced great deeds or
great poets, and it never will. Strong and
practically unanimous convictions and passionate
earnestness are wanted for those two products.
The convictions of the community are in a state
of pitiable flux, and its passions are queiscent,
save in the pursuit of puny personal objects. On
every conceivable subject the country is torn by
what we might call factions, if any of them had
vigour enough to deserve that name. What
wonder, then, if it can find no adequate voice,
no really one great poet, to give its feelings
utterance ? Its feelings are so complex and
unmarshalled that it requires a number of
small ambiguous voices to represent each
particular shade of its many moods and yearnings. It is not satisfied with anything, and
least of all is it satisfied with itself—only,
unfortunately, it lacks decision enough to be

thoroughly dissatisfied.   Could it arrive at that
culminating stage, it would then be possible for
a poet to arise to express a grand gigantic
discontent, and to indicate, to that extent, a
prospect of relief.   The opinions of everybody
who has thought on the subject at all invariably
conduct us to the same conclusion.   We do not
live in a culminating, comprehensive, adequate
epoch; and therefore we have not what Mr.
Matthew Arnold calls a culminating, comprehensive, and adequate literature.   Our poets do not
comprehend the situation, because it is so
illogical, self-conflicting, and chaotic, that possibly it cannot be comprehended.   We have

> "Infants crying in the night,
>   And with no language but a cry;"

but that obviously is not "adequate."   Turning
to Comte's theory, we are led to a similar issue;
for he merely states the same thing in different
words.   We have no concord, intellectual, moral,
social, or vital; and, accordingly, we waste our
puny individual or sectional efforts in letting off
a series of small fireworks.   We lack volume,
for combination alone can give that.

Listen to what another great French critic,

still living, says in corroboration of this same theory. "Il n'y à pas" (writes M. Ernest Renan, in his Essay on Lamennais) "de plus mauvaise disposition pour un philosophe et un critique que ce feu ardent et sombre, cette colère profonde et obstinée qui ne veut pas être adoucie; il n'y a pas de meilleure pour un artiste et un poète. Le tour absolu des opinions de Lamennais, qui nous a valu tant de pauvres raisonnements, tant de jugements défectueux, nous a valu aussi les cinquante pages de grand style les plus belles de notre siècle."*

Truer words were never penned; and they are strikingly applicable to the Poetry of the Period. Some of our poets, or would-be poets, are, as we have seen, very decent philosophers—. Mr. Browning remarkably so—and not bad reasoners; but they lack that *feu ardent et sombre* indispensable to the great singer. And the amusing part of it is, that the admirers of the

---

* "No worse disposition could there be for a philosopher and a critic than that ardent but sombre fire, that profound and obstinate anger, which will on no account be mollified; there could not possibly be a better one for an artist and a poet. To the absolute character of the opinions of Lamennais, to which we owe so much indifferent reasoning and so many defective judgments, we are indebted, however, for fifty pages, in the real grand style, which are the most beautiful of our time."

Poetry of the Period are so hopelessly astray in the matter, that they actually estimate poets by what they call their power of speculative thought; one journal much addicted to this sort of thing, rating Byron very cheaply, because, as is alleged, "he was a sheer Philistine in all matters of criticism." The "Philistinism," by the way, is alleged to be shown in admiration of Pope. I should be disposed to associate that term with an incapacity for admiring him. All this, however, is utterly beside the question; and I have alluded to it only to show how utterly at sea is the average mind of the time on the subject of poetry, and indeed of art of all kinds. No such tenth-rate authorities, however, carry any weight. It is to thinkers and scholars, like Mr. Arnold, M. Renan, and Comte that we must have recourse. "L'art a besoin d'un énergique parti pris," says M. Renan; and without that, all the philosophy, reasoning, and speculative powers in the world will avail a man nothing. The age, bemuddled and perplexed, is capable of no *parti pris*. Hamlet is its prototype. It is a mass of distracted irresolution, and is consequently powerless; and the curse of its impotence is upon each and every of its children.

It may possibly strike some people as arrogant thus to dispose of the pretensions of living poets, supported as they are by certain living critics. My answer is, that it is of no use having opinions without having also the courage of them; that I have long and deeply pondered the matter on which I have written; that false pretensions are an injury to literature, and to the honour of the mighty dead; that I have given plentiful quotations to enable my readers to judge for themselves; and that newspaper criticism has given some people such factitious authority that it is only fair and good work to set them down at their full value. Let us take but one instance, but it covers a multitude of others. I will begin with a quotation :—

SCENE II.

(*Adam alone.*)

Adam. " Misery, oh my misery ! O God, God !
    How could I ever, ever, could I do it ?
    Whither am I come ? where am I ? O me miserable !
    My God ! my God ! that I were back with Thee !
    O fool ! O fool ! O irretrievable act !
    Irretrievable what, I should like to know.

> What act, I wonder ?   What is it I mean ?
> Fool—Fool ! where am I ? O my God ! Fool
>   —fool !
> Why did we do 't ? Eve—Eve ! Where are you ?
>   Quick !
> O God ! O God ! what are we ? what shall we
>   do ?
> What is all this about, I wonder now.
> Yet I am better, too.   I think it will pass."

Now what do my readers think of that ? That it is simply idiotic drivel, of course. Nevertheless, they will find it quoted, no longer ago than the 11th of last September, in a review of the works of Arthur Hugh Clough, who is the writer of it ; the reviewer in terms of admiration, calling it " this remarkable soliloquy." On the same occasion, he declares that Clough has written " one of the greatest poems—if not in all English literature, which is likely enough— certainly of our day and generation." Is it arrogant to declare of such a critic that he is an ignorant and presumptuous scribbler, wholly unentitled to give an opinion on poetry at all ? Yet such contemptible stuff as the above is nowadays printed by the weekly cartload.

So much for the want of deference shown to individuals. As for the age itself, it should be remembered that every age is addicted to self-complacency, and this age of ours is not peculiarly free from that quality. Every age has had its great poets, until both the poets and the age were dead. "The fame of Ausonius," says Gibbon, "stamps the criticism of the time." Some future Gibbon will, I fear, make the same painful observation about our time and Mr. Tennyson. Locke professed a profound admiration for the genius of Sir Richard Blackmore; and the verses of Charles Montagu, Earl of Halifax, figure in various collections of the British classics. There have been times in English literature when a man writing of living poets could not well have omitted a reference to Nahum Tate, Laurence Eusden, Colley Cibber, William Whitehead, and Henry James Pye; for each of these now obscure worthies was, in his turn, Poet Laureate of England. Burns spoke of Shenstone as "the celebrated poet whose divine elegies do honour to our nation, our language, and our species." Yet, alas for the vanity of contemporary fame! when Hugh Miller visited the Leasowes, and asked in Halesowen for a copy of Shenstone's poems, the shopwoman had never heard of him; but she knew Samuel Salt, a local teetotal poet, and offered him a wrathful satire of Samuel's on the community of Oddfellows! So it is. *Nemo judex in sua causa;* no age can be trusted to assess its own merits and that of its poets. Posterity, that rude court of appeal, far oftener than not upsets such interested decisions; and it will certainly upset that which affects to talk of the bards of whom we have discoursed as great poets. "Faites grand, sire!" said an admirer lately to the Emperor of the French; but that is precisely what neither sovereign nor singer can in these days do. Many living writers of poetry have written beautifully and well, and some of their verse will for a time be kindly remembered. But they have fallen short of true greatness, and accordingly they will not be admitted among the stars that shine for ever and ever.

F. BENTLEY AND CO., PRINTERS, SHOE LANE, FLEET STREET, LONDON.